speaking in whispers

speaking in whispers

African-American Lesbian Erotica

by
Kathleen E. Morris

Third Side Press
Chicago

Copyright © 1996 by Kathleen E. Morris

All rights reserved. This book may not be reproduced in whole or in part, in any form or by any means, electronic or mechanical, including photocopying, recording, or by an information storage and retrieval system, except for the quotation of brief passages in reviews, without prior permission from Third Side Press, Inc.

This is a work of fiction. The events described here are imaginary; the settings and characters are fictitious and not intended to represent any specific places or persons.

"A Change of Seasons" is excerpted with permission from *For K* by Nerida Gil-Jimenez, 1991.

Printed on acid-free, recycled paper in the United States of America.

Library of Congress Cataloging-in-Publication Data
Morris, Kathleen E., 1962-
    Speaking in whispers : African-American lesbian erotica / by Kathleen E. Morris. — 1st ed.
      p. cm.
    ISBN 1-879427-28-1 (alk. paper)
    1. Afro-American lesbian—Sexual behavior—Fiction. 2. Lesbians' writings, American. 3. Erotic stories, American. I. title.
    PS3569.O874434S64   1996
    813'.54—dc20   96-222395
                                             CIP

Third Side Press
2250 W. Farragut
Chicago, IL 60625-1802

First edition, October 1996
10 9 8 7 6 5 4 3 2 1

To Nerida Gil-Jimenez—muse, teacher, and friend—whose warrior spirit, once upon a time, awakened mine in me—and whose spirit begins and weaves throughout this book.

And to Salem, my 18-pound PWA (Pussy With Attitude) who allows me space in his home.

CONTENTS

Acknowledgments	9
Introduction	10
Her	11
Lessons	15

Spring 25

Second Chances	27
The Movies	37
The Club	41

Autumn 51

The Painter	53
The Spa	61
Appetizers	77
The Festival	81

Summer 95

Honey Eyes	99
The Exit	103
Pongee	113

Winter 123

Honeymoon Cottage	125
The Gateway	151

A Change of Seasons

Yet, unlike flowers
   or wheat,
love needs not the Spring
to laugh with life . . .
   I know. . . .
For amidst starry, snowy nights
   I tasted Passion's fruit
and drank its nectar ripe. . .

—Nerida Gil-Jimenez

ACKNOWLEDGMENTS

Blessings to the many wimmin who have joined me in this journey—some as lovers, all as friends. Sharing with me in precious, sacred moments your lives, loves, dreams. On candlelit midnights, in sun-drenched dandelion fields of protest, sweating on the steaming pavement of inner city streets, whispering in dark corners of crowded clubs. You have touched my heart, my life (sometimes my breasts, my thighs, my . . .) and helped me grow into the womon I am—and will become.

I must shout out to the Universe some very special names—give voice to the spirits who have nurtured me and inspired me, endured my endless Libran equivocations and kicked my Gemini-rising ass—without which this book would not be in existence: Rosina Riley and Del Hornbuckle, Cheryl Minor, Linda Vitali, Peggy Lumpkin, Risë Shifra Shamansky, Tonya Smith, Aiku Williams, Pat Isaacs, and Betsy Koffman.

Also, to some of those still holding pieces of my heart: Bonita "Bean" Evans, Lynn Porter, Fran Davis, Deanna Johnson, Louise Phillips, and Alayna Woods Buffalo.

Finally, but certainly not lastly, I give thanks to my family who have always loved me and supported me, especially my mother, Carole Morris, and my sisters, Linda Lynch and Deborah Morris.

INTRODUCTION

Speaking in Whispers is a collection of erotic short stories that celebrates the diversity in shape, style, and manner of loving of African-American lesbians. At a conference I attended a few years back, a group of wimmin got to talking about their sex lives (or lack thereof). Once we got past the initial embarrassment and started talking frankly about our experiences, we found a common thread of basic dissatisfaction—primarily due to a lack of communication and imagination—with our lovers. We found that adherence to strict "roles" and fear of rejection/ridicule in confessing fantasies left us frustrated, angry, repressed. The erotic literature we read was generally vague and "pretty," the characters predominantly white, *and* the stories didn't really *move* us. We talked about how great it would be if someone wrote a book of erotica that "got to the point" clearly and unabashedly; that featured "us" as wimmin who loved *being* wimmin and loving wimmin—our scents, curves, idiosyncrasies—black wimmin who love wimmin because it is the natural expression of the love of our own feminine selves. Later, a friend encouraged me to try my hand at it. *Speaking in Whispers* is the result.

HER

Sheryl felt her face flush, her heart beat erratically in her chest. Someone was watching her. She could feel eyes burning through her tailored suit, touching the filmy lingerie beneath.

Yes, Sheryl could feel eyes boring into her, but she was afraid to look up. Afraid, because she knew who studied her so intently, who had discovered her secret.

Sheryl had seen HER board the train two stops back. A surreptitious look took in tailored trousers and yellow polo. The hair was worn closely cropped and natural—the way "they" were wearing it these days. In less than five seconds, Sheryl had imprinted all of this in her memory.

Fumbling in her purse, Sheryl pulled out a book and turned to the marked page. She rubbed her tired eyes, but still the words blurred together and refused to make sense as her thoughts returned to HER.

Although SHE wore a touch of blush and lipstick, as well as small silver balls in her ears, it was apparent, at least to Sheryl, not only what SHE was, but that SHE didn't care who else knew.

Sheryl forced herself to concentrate on her book—and had almost succeeded—when someone touched her arm. SHE was suddenly seated beside Sheryl, and as Sheryl gazed into HER eyes, SHE calmly, casually, placed HER hand lightly on Sheryl's linen-clad thigh.

Sheryl felt lightheaded as she stared at the hand. The skin was smooth and brown, the nails, short and unpainted, were well tended. There was a thin silver and turquoise ring on the pinky and another silver ring, with what looked like some kind of ax etched into it, on the middle finger. Slowly the hand turned, and Sheryl noted the long lifeline on the palm as the fingers curled closed over hers.

They exited the train at the next stop. A cloak of humid heat surrounded the two wimmin as they walked up West End Avenue. Sheryl's blouse clung to her as perspiration poured down her back and between her breasts. Her panties were damp too, though for a different reason. No words were exchanged between them, but Sheryl knew they were going to HER apartment.

She followed HER into the cool, large lobby of a beautifully restored, prewar building, and into the waiting elevator. SHE pushed the top floor button, and the doors shushed closed. With a low hum, the elevator began its ascent. SHE had been standing just behind Sheryl, and now SHE moved forward, pressing HER breasts against Sheryl's back.

Sheryl's body trembled as HER long fingers reached forward to stroke and pinch Sheryl's nipples, fondle her small, sensitive breasts.

Sheryl leaned back into HER and allowed HER to unbutton her blouse, hissing with pleasure as the cool air washed over her flaming skin, raising flesh bumps which SHE soothed with HER caress.

Sheryl closed her eyes, savoring HER warm breath, smelling of coffee and peppermint, on her neck and cheek.

SHE was murmuring words in Sheryl's ears in a language of desire that Sheryl had never heard before, though her body understood and responded to it passionately.

One of HER hands slipped up beneath Sheryl's skirt and played gently with the elastic edge of Sheryl's soaking panties before moving on to the soft hair and tender skin concealed beneath the wispy fabric.

SHE pushed Sheryl up against the paneled wall, and Sheryl gripped the cold, polished brass handrail, shuddering at the feel of the warm metal of HER rings against her skin as HER fingers rimmed Sheryl's thirsting canal. SHE squeezed Sheryl's breast in one hand, while HER other hand slowly pumped Sheryl, HER thumb manipulating Sheryl's pulsating clit. SHE was grinding hard against Sheryl's ass, harder, as HER excitement grew.

Sheryl moaned as she felt an orgasm threaten. "No, no—not yet." Sheryl whimpered. "Not here." But SHE wouldn't stop. Sheryl's body went rigid as a luxurious orgasm overwhelmed her.

Goddess! *This* is what Sheryl had always secretly craved—the feel, the heat of another womon. How had SHE known? Well, it didn't really matter now. Sheryl had had a taste and she wanted more.

Sheryl had to touch HER, to feel HER tongue in her mouth. Turning, Sheryl—

Looked up. The train slowed as it pulled into her station. Sheryl's heart was racing, her body throbbing. Oh god, had anyone noticed, she wondered, as she quickly surveyed the faces in the crowded subway car. Everyone looked tired or annoyed, frustrated or preoccupied, but no one was looking at her.

The train stopped. People began pushing toward the doors and Sheryl, unsteady on her feet, tumbled from the train.

As the doors closed, Sheryl chanced a final glance in HER direction. SHE was staring at Sheryl through the dirty glass, a secret smile on HER lips. SHE knew. Sheryl turned away quickly, blindly bumping into someone. Mumbling an apology, she raced home.

LESSONS

Loren was fuming. Her lover, Terri, had been showing out all night. Ignoring her except for an occasional snotty or macho remark tossed her way. Loren hated it when Terri hung out with this group, because she always felt compelled to become The Stone Butch Monster.

Terri was telling her friends a joke and they were doubled over in laughter. Loren watched Terri and thought darkly, "But you have to come home with me."

One of the other couples was arguing, and Terri and the others were snickering and passing comments. Then Terri reached over and put her arm around Loren's shoulders, pulling her possessively to her. When Loren didn't resist, as she usually did, a look of smug satisfaction crossed Terri's face.

"See?" Terri nudged her friend. "*My* womon knows how to behave. Don't you baby?"

Oh really? Loren smiled and said nothing. It was fine for now. But later? We'll just see who knows how to behave. Oh yeah, Loren could hardly wait.

λ λ λ

Terri dropped the keys on the table and slammed the door behind them.
Loren turned to her. "Shhh! Keep it down. It's late."
Terri glared at her. "Oh—what's this attitude? Are you trying to order me around?"
It was all Loren could do to keep her voice calm. She answered, "I'm sorry honey. I'm just tired."
Terri slumped in her chair. "Well, okay. That's better. Come give me a kiss."
Loren crossed to Terri and sat on her lap, giving her a long, passionate kiss. Terri held her close, stroking her thigh, pushing her dress up to reveal the tops of her gartered stockings.
"You're so soft baby," Terri breathed into Loren's neck. "God, I love how you feel."
Loren rubbed her breasts seductively against Terri. She parted her thighs, straddling Terri's trousered lap.
Terri fingered the fabric covering Loren's pussy, her breathing becoming more labored.
"Come on—let's go to bed. I've been wanting to fuck you all night."
Loren stood, unbuttoning her blouse. "I need to take a shower first, okay?" She headed toward the back as she removed her shirt and dropped it on the floor. At the door she turned, slipping her bra off as she spoke.

"Why don't you join me? I'll be your geisha—I know how much you like that."

Terri's eyes were locked on the brown circles of Loren's breasts as she stood and moved toward her, stripping quickly. They made their way to the bathroom.

They stepped into the tub and closed the curtain. Loren, bending to turn on the water, pressed her ass up against Terri. She took her time adjusting the temperature, allowing Terri to press and grind against her. This would be easier than she'd thought, Loren smiled to herself as she turned on the shower and stood against Terri, the water washing over them and filling the room with steam.

Picking up the soap, Loren started sudsing Terri's body. Her hands slipped over Terri's muscled arms, over and under her heavy breasts, and down sturdy thighs. Loren slid her hand between those thighs, lathering the wiry black hairs and the soft folds hidden beneath.

Loren worked slowly, carefully building Terri's passion. Her own body throbbed in anticipation of her plans.

Her fingers gently rocked Terri's swelling clit. With a groan of lust, Terri urged Loren to her knees.

Loren gripped Terri's ass as she locked her mouth on Terri's center. Terri held Loren's head, dictating the speed and pressure she needed for satisfaction. The water cascaded over the two wimmin, warm drops mixing with Terri's cream as Loren sucked her.

Loren could feel the tension in Terri's powerful body build as Terri neared orgasm. She increased the speed and pressure of her lapping tongue as Terri came.

They got out of the shower and, still wet, went into the bedroom. Terri flopped on the bed, eyes closed.

"Damn baby. That felt so good. Let me lie here a second and calm down a little. Umph. I'm gonna fuck you so good. . . ." Moments later, she was snoring lightly.

Loren smiled wickedly as she watched Terri sleep for a minute. Then she went to her dresser drawer and pulled out several scarves.

Carefully, so as not to awaken her, Loren tied Terri's wrists and ankles securely to the bed posts before reaching under the bed for Terri's little bag. When everything was ready, she shook Terri roughly.

"Wake up you inconsiderate bitch."

"Wha—what the hell?!" Terri strained against the scarves. "What do you think you're doing?"

"I think it's time for a refresher course on how to treat your womon." Loren said as she crossed the room and turned on the stereo.

"You've been begging for this for a while." Loren closed the bedroom door. "So I've decided to give it to you."

"Let me up! I don't play this shit!" Terri howled.

"You play what I tell you to play. I don't usually mind your doing the 'butch thing' in public, but you got completely out of hand tonight—ordering me around, showing off in front of your friends. Did you really think I would let you get away with that? Now we'll just see who's in charge." Loren picked up a long, fluffy pink feather and started flicking it lightly over Terri's naked body.

"Stop it! Let me loose!" Terri giggled/shouted. "I'm not playing with . . . ha! ha! . . . you, dammit!!!" Terri rocked and bucked on the mattress, but she succeeded only in tightening her restraints more. Loren leaned over and pinched one of Terri's erect nipples until Terri groaned.

"Now you quiet down and stop threatening me." Loren held the nub a moment longer, and then released it, trailing her hand down to Terri's crotch.

She stroked Terri's exposed inner thighs softly, and then ran a finger along Terri's slit, holding up her now shiny digit for Terri's inspection. "I think you liked that, didn't you?" Loren teased.

Terri's brow drew together angrily. "Fuck you, Loren. When I get up . . ."

Loren smiled. "Are you threatening me again? You know, I don't think I like your attitude. Oh well," she sighed, "I guess I'll just have to adjust it."

Loren took out a small vibrator and switched it on. She ran it slowly over Terri's mound. Terri twitched involuntarily.

"Oooh . . . do you like that? Hummmmm?" Loren moved the toy slowly down Terri's pussy, pausing it on her sensitive button. Terri strained to avoid the contact, but she was helpless.

Feeling an orgasm quickly spreading through her limbs, Terri gave in to it—but at the crucial moment, Loren removed the vibrator, leaving Terri frustrated and throbbing.

"You don't deserve to cum yet." Loren advised her. "You haven't learned your lesson."

Loren straddled Terri and placed the vibrator against her own pussy. She manipulated it slowly, throwing her head back and arching her back invitingly. She closed her eyes to slits, watching through her lashes as Terri licked her lips hungrily. Loren knew Terri loved watching her pleasure herself. Loren pulled and squeezed her breasts with her free hand until she came. Then, tossing the vibrator aside, she wiped her pulsing cunt slowly over Terri's face, drenching her with her cum.

Loren lay on Terri, pussy to pussy, and whispered, "You want to cum, don't you?" She ground Terri's steaming mound and Terri, despite herself, moaned.

"Admit you like me fucking you like this. You like lying on your back, helpless, while I fuck you, don't you?"

Loren pinched Terri's nipples hard, smiling when Terri arched her back and groaned. "You can tell me—it will be our secret. Come on BUTCH, ask your femme to let you cum. Let me hear you say *PLEASE.*"

Terri bit her lip, shaking her head and closing her eyes.

Loren laughed. "Aren't you macho." She put her hands on either side of Terri's head, forcing her to look up.

Terri's eyes were filled with lust, but stubborn pride kept her mouth clamped shut.

Loren got up. "Well, you've had your chance to play nicely, to ask for what you *know* you want, but you are just too damn stubborn, so I guess I'll have to take it." Loren chatted conversationally as she went into the closet. When she emerged, she was wearing Terri's harness and dildo.

Terri's eyes widened in shock. "Okay—okay, you've made your point. I was an asshole, okay? Is that what you want me to say?"

Loren walked slowly toward Terri, the black rod bouncing ominously in front of her. "I don't think you're *really* sorry."

"Hey—stop! You're going too far! I don't like getting fucked. I don't play that shit!"

"Shut up." Loren hissed. "I told you before—you play what I tell you to play. And *I* say you need to be more thoroughly fucked than anyone I know."

She stood over Terri. "And you're going to like it." Loren straddled Terri's body again and started licking and sucking Terri's neck, which never failed to turn Terri on. Terri gasped as Loren's lips traced down her belly, her chin pressing against Terri's pussy. Then Loren moved back up, driving Terri mad with the insistent rubbing of the dildo between her thighs. Loren poked it around the rim of Terri's soaking pussy and Terri's traitorous cunt reached up to draw it inside. Loren chuckled, pulling away and continued teasing Terri's pulsating hole.

"You want it, don't you?" Loren teased. "Go ahead. Say you want it."

Terri bit her lip and said nothing.

Loren pushed the dildo slowly into Terri.

Terri moaned as Loren withdrew it.

"Say you want it."

Terri looked pleadingly up at Loren.

"Uh, uh. That's not good enough."

Loren stuffed the rod up inside Terri, grinding pussy to pussy for a few moments before withdrawing, rubbing the slick member along Terri's stomach.

"Tell me that you want me to fuck you." Loren let the head slip just inside again.

Terri lifted her pelvis. "Please," she whispered.

Loren smiled, pushing the dildo further in. "Say, 'fuck me, Loren'." She pushed it in more, moved it around. A tear dropped from Terri's eye. "... me." Terri panted. Loren pumped her harder. "I didn't hear you." She reached down and pinched Terri's swollen, throbbing clit.

"Oh god—fuck me! Fuck me, goddamn it!"

Loren gripped the bed posts for leverage, digging her toes into the bed as she pumped Terri. Loren jabbed and withdrew, jamming Terri's throbbing center.

"Yesss... ah... yes... ah baby!" Terri cried as Loren locked on, filling Terri's hole, grinding her pussy until Terri's bucking body stiffened, an orgasm slamming through her.

"Oh shit!... fuck... oh damn!..." Terri cursed as Loren wrung the last drops of pleasure from her.

Terri fell back weak, spent. Loren kissed her nose and then pulled out. She untied Terri's hands and then rolled over into her arms. Terri held her tightly.

They fell asleep.

λ λ λ

The first thing Loren noticed the next morning when she awoke was that the harness and dildo had been removed. Then she smelled coffee and fresh biscuits. She sat up, rubbing her eyes as Terri came in carrying a tray. She set the tray beside Loren and sat on the edge of the bed.

"I thought you might like breakfast in here for a change."

Loren took in the carefully arranged basket of biscuits, plate of crispy bacon surrounding a perfect omelet. A pot of coffee and a pitcher of freshly squeezed orange juice flanked a vase containing a yellow tulip and a cloud of baby's breath as a final, special touch.

Picking up a biscuit, Loren imperiously smeared honey on it. Then, taking a bite, she looked up at Terri. "Well, it looks like you've really learned your lesson, huh?"

Terri smiled as she munched on a strip of bacon. "Oh yes. But you know me and my memory. If I should slip up, I guess you'll just have to teach me again."

SPRING

It took me forty minutes to climb the path to Look Out Point. I am sitting on the stone ledge, looking out over the land, struggling to regain my breath. Was the trail so steep before? I feel silly being here—it's been so long since . . . I'd hoped—but didn't really expect you to have remembered.

The land is unchanged after all these years, but I am older—not as quick or resilient as I was that April when we met. The ground today is covered with patches of snow, but I recall it being sunny and dry, then. I am wearing a heavy sweater over my flannel shirt, also thermals and gloves. I don't remember it being so cold, do you? Still, the air is bracing. I feel alive. I can smell the earth and new life on the icy breeze. That was your scent—fresh and natural.

It's been ten years—today's our anniversary. For one brief but beautiful season we loved—and then I lost you—life's cruel joke. You said you'd come back. Do you even remember me?

I am a little heavier, my dark hair is now sprinkled with—wisdom. I have loved and been loved, though I am alone right now.

Ahh! There is the path to our clearing. Surely you remember that—where we made love that first day. We laid our jackets down on the spongy moss and stripped—except for our flannel shirts—the one I'm wearing today. You had a little tattoo on your left breast—an emerald green serpent twisting around your nipple. I thought you so racy! Oh, you *loved* having your toes sucked—you kept them manicured just in case you got lucky. Remember? So bold you were!

I was shy—my first time with a womon. You opened me gently, slowly, like a delicate flower, careful not to bruise my petals. I felt newborn that spring. That was your gift to me.

I am heading down the path, wondering if our place is still there—or if some person, unaware that it is our sacred grotto—has put up picnic tables, or cut down our tree. Just around the bend. A little further.

There is someone there. Sitting against our tree, eating an apple. An older womon wearing—a flannel shirt. She looks up and smiles.

"I was hoping that you would come," she says.

It's you.

SECOND CHANCES

Jaime turned from the window. The moonlight cut through the shadows of the room and illuminated the form lying in the bed, blanket clutched protectively in clenched fists. Tears welled in Jaime's eyes as she watched the blanket rise and fall in the gentle, steady rhythm of sleep. She sat on the edge of the bed and looked at the peaceful face of her lover.

Tonya's eyes fluttered beneath lids smudged with shadow; her full lips moved slightly, as if in answer to the secret dialogue of dreams. Jaime smoothed her lover's hair and lightly brushed the skin of her shoulder. She touched the beads of perspiration that gathered between Tonya's breasts. Gently cupping a breast in her hand, Jaime felt its fullness, its ripeness. She watched the nipples harden in anticipation of a lover's kiss.

Jaime had come so close to losing this precious womon. Moving back to the window, Jaime watched the cars make their way through the snow-covered streets of predawn Manhattan. There was so much of life that Jaime had missed after Anne, her partner of fifteen years, had died three years ago. Jaime had believed she could never fall in love again, would never make the kind of commitment or have the level of trust that she and Anne had shared.

So Jaime had packed her heart away, pouring all of her energies into her restaurant. Though she dated occasionally and attended parties from time to time, no one had been able to penetrate the walls of her lonely prison.

And then she met Tonya at a cocktail party. Beautiful, talented, brilliant Tonya. Tonya. Who'd brought laughter back into her life.

Tonya. Who'd offered Jaime her youthful enthusiasm for life, her loving attention and unconditional friendship. They spent time together—walks in Central Park, visits to museums and galleries, forays to movies and alternative music events. They spent Sunday afternoons having brunch in Upper West Side bistros or on the floor of Jaime's living room sipping coffee and reading the comics. When Jaime looked back, even now, she could find no uncomfortable moments, no awkward lingering when they parted company. They were both seemingly content with each other's companionship.

It was snowing again. A plow made its noisy way down the street in a futile attempt to clear it. Jaime's breath clouded the window, and she drew a happy face in the mist before turning and leaving the bedroom. She headed for the kitchen to put the kettle on to boil. Jaime smiled as she sat at the table. Her friends had questioned her endlessly about the new womon in her life.

Jaime had brushed their sly comments and queries away with an impatient wave her hand. "Don't be ridiculous—we're just friends. She's *way* too young for me."

So when had it changed? Jaime turned the fire off and poured water into her mug. She took her steaming cup back to the table and sipped cautiously.

Tonya's trip must have been the turning point. She had been attending a conference for a week, and when she returned, Jaime had picked her up at the airport, inviting her over for a welcome-home dinner.

Jaime prepared some of Tonya's favorites: mahimahi, baked with shallots and lemon, served on a bed of couscous and surrounded by slender stems of tender asparagus. When the meal was done, Tonya suggested they have dessert and coffee in the den. Sitting on the floor, their backs against the sofa, a fire warming their toes, they enjoyed Jaime's freshly prepared tropical fruit salad, topped with a mango yogurt dressing. They finished off with brandy-laced espressos.

It was a magical evening. They laughed and joked. Tonya fed morsels of plump, juicy fruit to Jaime, and Jaime massaged her feet. And then—it happened.

Tonya leaned forward, whispering something and giggling at her silliness. Her face was just inches from Jaime's, her lips moist and full. Jaime could not resist the urge to kiss that sweet mouth, and Tonya responded, returning the kiss passionately.

Tonya's hands held Jaime's face, and Jaime felt herself melting into Tonya. She caught herself, pushing roughly away from Tonya and standing unsteadily on her feet. Tonya looked up at her, confusion and hurt marking her brow.

"What's wrong? Did I do something?"

Jaime turned away and said, "I don't know why I did that. I didn't mean to . . ." and turning back, "This can't happen. I'm—I'm so sorry. Excuse me."

Jaime fled to the bathroom and splashed cold water on her face, trying to calm herself. When she returned, Tonya was gone.

λ λ λ

Jaime had tried calling Tonya that night and the next morning, but Tonya's machine was on and she did not return Jaime's calls. The week was almost over before Jaime heard from her. Tonya sounded cool and formal. She asked Jaime to meet her for dinner. They needed to talk.

At the restaurant, Jaime tried to engage in friendly banter, but Tonya remained silent, refusing to be drawn in. Finally, Jaime gave up and watched the waiter take her half-eaten dinner away.

They were ordering coffee and dessert when Tonya finally spoke, briskly. "I don't think we should spend so much time together anymore." Jaime studied Tonya's face but could not read its expression.

"Why? What is it that I've done?"

Tonya eyes suddenly reflected pain and disappointment. "You haven't done anything. And that's my problem. You haven't done anything at all."

Jaime was confused. "I thought we were getting along so well. I apologized for taking advantage of you the other night. I don't know what else you want from me."

Tonya leaned forward. "Do you really want to know what I want?" Jaime nodded and Tonya continued.

"I . . . I want to make love to you, Jaime. I want to wake up tomorrow morning in your arms. I can't pretend anymore that I don't want more than just your friendship."

Tonya looked down at the table, brushing imaginary crumbs from the cloth and added softly, "I will accept your friendship if that is really all you want to give me. But I'll need a little time. I think I've fallen in love with you."

Jaime was stunned. She hadn't realized how much she had wanted to hear Tonya say those words, how long she had wanted to say them to Tonya. She turned them over and over in her head. "She loves me. She loves me."

Tonya was looking shyly at Jaime. "I need you to tell me how you feel. Or at least tell me this—do I have a chance with you?"

Until that very moment, Jaime had not admitted, even to herself, how very connected to Tonya she had become—how in the middle of the day she found herself lost in the memory of Tonya's scent, the feel of Tonya's head on her shoulder as they talked into the early hours, the way Tonya's lips felt on her cheek when they kissed good night. And Jaime shivered with excitement even now, at the thought of making love to her.

But Jaime had always pushed those thoughts aside. Somehow she had always known that if she made love to Tonya her heart would be lost, irretrievably. She had fully believed that she would never, could never, make love to another womon after Anne. She had, for so long, believed that it was not possible for her to feel that way about another womon.

Focusing back on the present, Jaime turned to Tonya but, with eyes filled with tears, Tonya had run from the table. Jaime threw some money on the table and took off after her.

She caught Tonya at the corner and grabbed her by the arm as she was about to cross the street. Tears streaked Tonya's cheeks as Jaime folded her into her arms.

"Oh baby, yes, yes you have a chance. You have more than a chance. I didn't think I could ever want anyone as much as I want you now."

Tonya pulled away and, wiping her tears, smiled shakily. "Then let's go to my place."

λ λ λ

Jaime's heart was pounding as they entered Tonya's dark apartment. She dropped her coat on the sofa and crossed the room as Tonya locked the door behind them.

Tonya dropped her keys on the table and kicked off her shoes. She padded over to Jaime, stopping a few feet away. They stood that way, in semidarkness for a moment, the full moon throwing a beam of light through the partially opened drapes.

A soft breeze came through the window, brushing strands of hair across Tonya's face. Jaime watched Tonya shrug off her coat and let it drop to the floor.

Tonya's eyes never wavered from Jaime's, nor did she utter a sound as she reached behind her, unzipped her dress, and stepped out of it.

Jaime watched transfixed, as Tonya's pendant, resting in the hollow between her breasts, rose and fell with each breath. Tonya's nipples were hard and pressing against the fabric of her bra, her full breasts straining to be freed.

Tonya turned on the stereo and then stepped closer to Jaime as she unsnapped the clasp of her lacy binding. She pressed her nearly naked body against Jaime's, seductively grinding her pelvis against Jaime's as she whispered huskily, "Let's dance."

There were no other sounds in the room but the hissing of steam escaping from the radiator and the soft music from the stereo as they danced.

Jaime closed her eyes and gave in to the sensation of each note washing over her, finally finding its place in a puddle of warm wetness between her legs.

Jaime held her breath as Tonya slowly brushed her lips across Jaime's eyelids, cheeks, the corners of her mouth. She held her breath as Tonya softly traced the outlines of her face with her fingertips before leaning forward to kiss Jaime fully on the lips.

Tonya pushed Jaime's hands away when Jaime tried to pull Tonya to her, and she pressed Jaime against the wall. Tonya's hands reached beneath Jaime's shirt and sighed with pleasure as she reached for, and found, Jaime's breasts. She squeezed and pressed Jaime's tender nipples, and as she moved down to suckle them, Tonya kneaded the muscles of Jaime's naked back. Again, Jaime tried to reach for

Tonya, and again Tonya pushed her away, silencing Jaime's protest with a deep, probing kiss.

Every nerve ending on Jaime's body quivered. Jaime marveled that she was already teetering on the edge of orgasm.

Slowly, Tonya unbuttoned Jaime's shirt, lightly kissing the soft skin beneath as she revealed it to the moon-drenched room. Tonya moved slowly, inexorably downward, and Jaime gasped when Tonya finally moved her hand between Jaime's trousered thighs.

Tonya moaned softly, her mouth hungrily seeking every inch of Jaime's sweet flesh as she undressed her. Jaime leaned into Tonya, her hands pressing Tonya's face against her throbbing center.

Jaime had never allowed a woman to control her body as Tonya was now doing. She held her breath as Tonya unzipped her slacks, her lips hot on Jaime's burning skin.

Giving herself over, Jaime closed her eyes as Tonya undressed her. There was no place Tonya left untouched by hands or mouth, and Jaime blossomed beneath Tonya's ministrations. She felt as if she were a virgin, discovering pleasures of her body she had never explored, realizing emotions she never imagined could be tapped by another human being.

Tonya's mouth never left Jaime's body as the two wimmin slid down to the floor in front of the window. Jaime brushed the damp strands of hair from Tonya's neck and arched her back with a gasp as Tonya devoured her. Tonya was everywhere tasting, nibbling, driving Jaime mad with desire.

Almost faint from the intense sensations, Jaime alternately begged Tonya to stop and pleaded with her to go on, and Tonya continued to ignite her. Tonya scorched Jaime's flaming mound with her hand, and when Jaime shuddered with barely contained craving, she found Jaime's fragrant center. She dipped her tongue into Jaime's nectar and took her pulsing button into her mouth. She fed hungrily on Jaime's fleshy lips, pulling and nibbling, until Jaime felt as if she would be consumed in the fire of Tonya's desire. Finally, Tonya replaced her mouth with her hand and slowly, lovingly, quenched Jaime's fire.

Tonya stripped and positioned herself over Jaime, smiling when she saw Jaime flush at the heady scent of Tonya's arousal. Tonya pressed her soaking pussy down on Jaime's face, but when Jaime reached forward to feed hungrily, Tonya held her down. She slowly rubbed her pulsating cunt slowly across Jaime's face.

Tonya watched Jaime love her, which turned Jaime on tremendously. Jaime felt the tingling in her own center begin again, spreading slowly through her body.

Jaime moved with Tonya's rhythm: faster, slower she sucked and lashed at Tonya's pussy. And when Tonya's body heaved in orgasm, Jaime's body exploded into a thousand shards of light.

Tonya collapsed beside Jaime, and they lay clasped together in a pool of sweat. The breeze from the window cooled their bodies, and finally their breathing slowed.

Jaime rose up on one elbow and looked at Tonya's dozing face which was glowing with happiness. She kissed Tonya's eyelids and traced the tranquil face of her beloved. Then, slowly, she extricated herself from Tonya's arms and, trying not to awaken her, went to get a blanket from the bed.

When she returned, Tonya was sitting drowsily against the wall beneath the window, hair tousled, eyes heavy. Jaime smiled as Tonya rose from the floor and moved into her arms. They hugged for a moment, and then Jaime led Tonya into the bedroom.

THE MOVIES

The lights go out and the previews begin. A hand—soft, manicured—inches over to caress the strong, dark hand beside it. Fingers intertwine and squeeze acknowledgment of a lover's possession.
The film starts. Voices, images flickering. She leans over and whispers, "I'm feeling really turned on." With a smile she turns back to the screen, catching her partner's look of surprise in a sideways glance.
"Can I have some popcorn?" Her eyes never leave the screen, but she knows her lover watches as she licks the tiny, salty granules from her fingers. She whispers, "I wish you could lick me like this, right now."
A hand rests on bare thigh, gently.
"Oooh, god! I am so wet baby. Feel how wet I am."
A low groan, as the hand slides higher up the silky limb. Leaning over, nuzzling a smooth jaw she whispers, "I want you to touch me, right now."

Leg drapes over denim, parting thighs, inviting entry.

Slick fingers, low moan.

"Do you want to fuck me, honey?"

Husky whispered response, "Yes."

Cars chase across celluloid, vague dialogue, explosions. Teasing whisper, "What would you like to do to me? Tell me. I want you to tell me."

Seat shifts as a hand rises higher to a warmer, moister space. "I want to take you home right now. Press you up against the front door and crush you to me as I take you in my arms. And when you wrap one of those big thighs around me so that your soaking pussy is pressed against mine, I'll dip my fingers into you and tease you—plunging gently in and out, flickering around that sweet hole until you scream for release. You're gonna cry out baby—loud enough to echo in the hallways for all the neighbors to hear—cry out for me to take you. And I will. I'll throw you on the couch, rip that damn dress off of you, and take you.

"I'll grip your ass to me and grind you, sucking on your neck and marking your skin with my teeth until you cum all over our nice white sofa."

Wet hair curls around fingers that stroke slick skin, slippery, swelling folds.

Head on shoulder muffles moan in starched cotton. Deep, ragged breath. Control. Control.

Characters on screen dance naked, sweat on tangled white sheets. Music, voices from hidden speakers blend with heated sighs in the dark.

Slender fingers undo buttons on shirt. Scarlet nails trace lines, fondle fleshy breasts. Lips, tongue on jaw whispers, "And then?"

One hand puts popcorn on the floor as the other slips into a deeper, tighter darkness. Muscles flex, thumb rotates—slowly.

"Ahhh . . . ohhh. . . ." Sweet tingling. Bodies shift closer. Small hand squeezes denim thighs. Hand roams up, palm presses hard against soft center. Hips grind, fingers pump.

". . . baby . . ."

"Shhh. And then *I* am going to undress *you*, move slowly down your body—licking, biting, tasting until I reach your throbbing pussy. I'm going to bury my face there and suck you and lash you. I'm going to keep you on the edge—you'll go out of your mind before I take you over—plunging my tongue up and into you as I rim your ass. Oh baby, you are going to come like a tidal wave and drown me."

Faster and faster the hero flies across the screen. Faster and faster hands fly in aisle 23.

"Oh, baby . . ." Bodies slip down, lower, lower.

"Uh . . . umm . . . what about the movie?" gasping, aching.

"Forget it. We can catch it on video."

THE CLUB

Heavy bass pumped. Lights—red, yellow, blue—pulsed erratically, making the bodies swaying in the smoky haze of the dance floor seem dreamlike.

Tita stood at the entryway, legs spread apart, arms folded across her double-breasted chest, surveying the wimmin. She was there tonight for one reason—and one reason only—to pick out the hottest femme—and have her.

She knew she looked good. Her tawny skin glowed against the sable fabric of her tailored suit. The wool worsted did not disguise Tita's hard, muscled arms. The pants, cut full and tapering revealed bulging thighs—and something else. Tita grinned as her hand moved down, adjusting her equipment. Yeah. She was looking for action and she would have—HER.

Across the room, standing in the shadows of the bar was an ebony queen, dressed in a snug, beaded black mini. Her dark hair was pulled up, revealing a long, graceful neck, adorned by a silver chainlink choker. A hint of cleavage peeked above the rounded neckline of the dress, the skin glistened with tiny beads of sweat. She was talking to someone—laughing and sipping a drink.

She looked up and caught Tita's eye. Solemnly parting her full, crimson-colored lips, the woman fished out an ice cube from her drink and sucked it gently, her eyes never straying from Tita's. Then she took the cube and rubbed it over and between the swell of her breasts before turning back with a teasing half-smile to her companion and their discussion.

Tita adjusted her jacket and brushed an imaginary speck of lint from her lapel. With a low, hunter's growl, she stalked across the floor, stopping directly in front of the woman.

The woman's companion looked up, question on her face, but Tita ignored her, holding her hand out to the woman. Confusion turned to anger, and the companion started to speak, but the woman restrained her and took Tita's hand. Turning away, Tita's triumphant glance flickered across the stunned, jilted loser, and then dismissed her.

They moved to the center of the dance floor. Tita snaked her arm around the woman's waist, pulling her closer. The woman gasped in surprise as she brushed the hard bulge beneath Tita's belt and then moved closer, resting her head on Tita's shoulder. Her warm breath on Tita's neck and her gyrations against Tita's pelvis had Tita's pussy throbbing.

The music slowed and Tita slowed their movements down to a deep grind. She pressed her leg between the woman's, hiking up the dress and revealing the lacy garter straps on the woman's heavy, black-stockinged thigh. Tita slid her hand up the woman's leg, feeling the nylon, the skin above the stocking's edge and—hot cream clinging to—yes—the womon was not wearing underwear. Tita could feel her wetness in the tangle of silky hairs.

"Goddamn!" Tita growled, "Enough. Let's go." She turned and left the dance floor, pulling the womon with her.

λ λ λ

The night was cool—goosebumps rose on the womon's arms and Tita gallantly draped her jacket over the womon's shoulders.

"Where are we going?" the womon asked.

"Not far." Tita replied, as they headed into the parking lot.

They moved swiftly past the rows of cars, stopping beside a burgundy van. Tita reached into her pants pocket and fished out her keys. Deactivating the alarm, Tita opened the sliding side door and, putting a strong hand on the womon's elbow, helped her in. She followed, quickly closing and locking the door behind her.

It was dark in the van and Tita could hear the womon breathing—quick sips of air, filled with anticipation—and a little fear. Tita's pussy pulsed.

A sudden flash of light as Tita lit two cigarettes. She drew deeply and then passed one to the womon who took it with a slightly trembling hand. Tita then reached over and lit a candle, filling the cabin with golden light.

The womon looked around the well-appointed space. Tita was seated in one of two swivel captain chairs upholstered in gray leather. Between those chairs was a well-stocked bar and a little refrigerator. She was herself seated on a folded futon pushed up against the back wall of the van. Soft, overstuffed pillows were tossed haphazardly in a corner. She turned back to Tita who was busy pouring them drinks.

"Do you have music?" the womon asked as Tita handed her a frosted glass.

Tita pressed a button on the padded board beside her, and they were immediately surrounded by jazz saxophone.

"Well," the womon started as she sipped her drink, "this is certainly cozy."

Tita swallowed her drink, eyes narrowed, and said nothing.

"Um . . . I've . . . I've never been in a van . . . before. How long have you been . . . ?"

"I want you to take your clothes off now. Slowly, so I can watch."

The womon stuttered, "Hey, relax, what's the hurry? Let's have our drinks first—and talk a little."

Tita put her drink down and leaned forward. Gently caressing the womon's face, Tita said quietly, "I said, get undressed. I didn't bring you here to talk."

The womon's eyes, rimmed with long, mascara'd lashes, widened in surprise, but after a beat, she put her drink down, reached behind her, and started unzipping her dress.

Tita's heart was pounding, but her voice remained cool and steady. "No, not like that. Do it here."

The woman moved to where Tita had indicated. Again, she reached behind her to find the zipper and this time Tita didn't interrupt.

The woman let the sheath fall to the floor, her copper shadowed eyes lowered modestly.

Tita was glad the woman wasn't looking because, bringing her glass up for a sip, Tita had missed her mouth completely, sprinkling drops of wine down the front of her shirt. Her control was unraveling as she watched the woman slowly reveal her beautiful body.

The woman was wearing a black, lacy push-up camisole, one that almost—but did not quite—cover her large, ripe breasts. Tita's mouth watered as she took in the perfect orbs, the nipples a sweet plum color. The stockings were attached to garter straps on the camisole which ended in a lacy V, trimmed by the woman's own more luscious V of black fur.

Trying to stay calm, but with a voice thickening with passion, Tita said, "Now turn and take your hair down."

The woman turned slowly, revealing the taut, flawless skin of her voluptuous ass. She reached up and began removing the pins that held her French twist in place. Tita watched the muscles in the womon's back move and struggled to keep herself in check as the womon shook free her mane of curly black hair.

"Now get on your hands and knees so I can fuck you." Tita said roughly.

The womon swung around. "No. I've had enough." She picked up her dress and held it against her like a shield. With a pleading look in her eyes she said, "I want to go back to the club. I've . . . I've changed my mind."

Tita slid from her chair and knelt before the womon. She took the dress from her and tossed it aside. Then she stroked the womon's pussy and brought her hand, slick with its wetness, up to the womon's face.

"You don't really want to leave," Tita whispered, "do you?"

The womon's eyes lowered, "No."

Tita smiled and kissed the womon's forehead. "Then get on your hands and knees like I told you to. Right now." Tita returned to her chair as the womon complied.

Tita reached under her chair and pulled out a small leather paddle. She caressed the womon's ass with it, talking as if to herself. "I don't like being disobeyed. You need to learn to act without question." With that, Tita smacked the womon's ass and then continued caressing the reddening flesh.

"You do want to please me don't you?" Thwack! This time harder. "Don't you?"

The womon whimpered, "Yes."

"You like when I spank that sweet ass, don't you?" Tita brought the paddle down again.

The womon flinched.

"Don't you." Again and again.

"Yes. Yes, I like it," the womon cried.

"Good." Tita was rubbing her hand in semicircles over the womon's soft skin, hot thighs.

"Good. You're a good girl. I want you to be satisfied, too. I know what you need."

Tita slipped two fingers into the womon's now dripping cunt. The womon rocked back onto Tita's hand as Tita slowly finger-fucked her for a few moments. When Tita withdrew her fingers and sat back, the womon moaned hungrily.

"We have time for that later sweetie, but first, I want you to meet your host for the evening." The womon turned and stared as Tita unzipped her pants and pulled out her strap-on.

It was thick, veined, and dark chocolate brown. Tita ran her hand up from its base to the head and then reached into her inside jacket pocket and pulled out a condom. Tossing it to the womon, Tita said, "Take this. Put it on me."

The womon's eyes never left the phallic toy as she moved forward. She opened the little packet and, with trembling fingers, slipped the latex sleeve over Tita's "host."

Tita's hands were in the womon's hair, twisting, stroking. She pulled the womon close and kissed her hard—tonguing deep, exploring.

The womon responded eagerly, her painted fingernails tracing lines on Tita's back. Tita pushed the womon away, panting, trying to regain her composure. She moved, her back to the womon, and undressed. Then turning, she said, "Kiss it." Tita caught the womon's hair again and pulled her face to her lap.

The womon, tentative at first, kissed and then licked her "host." A satisfied grunt from Tita emboldened the womon and she rubbed the soft, hard member across and between her breasts, watching for Tita's reaction.

Tita's eyes were clouded with desire, and suddenly, the womon felt a surge of power. Tita liked what she was doing to her. Extending it out so Tita could better see what she was doing, the womon ran her tongue up and down the shaft. She circled the head and then swallowed half of the rod down her throat.

At the same time, she lightly stroked Tita's inner thigh, fingered the leather harness and pulled it lightly, putting more friction and pressure on Tita's clit. Tita moaned, tightening her grip on the womon's hair for a moment and then let her go, pushing the womon to the futon.

The womon got on her hands and knees, ass high in the air, welcoming Tita, who slid into her from behind and began pumping.

Sighs of fulfillment turned into frenzied pants as Tita, fucking her harder and faster, reached forward to play with the womon's engorged, hooded jewel, her other hand filled with the womon's heavy breast, nipple hard and pressing against the palm of Tita's hand.

"Ahh! . . . Ahhh! . . . God . . . oh . . . baby . . . Ahhh!" the womon rocked back with a jolt, cumming in waves.

After a moment, Tita turned her over and entered from the front.

Stroking her in long pulls, Tita whispered to the womon, "You like getting fucked, don't you, baby? You're a hot little bitch and you love getting fucked, don't you?" Tita stroked faster, her face flush with excitement.

"Yes, baby. I love it. I love how you're giving it . . . to . . . me!" The womon clutched Tita's ass, pulling her closer.

Tita felt herself losing it. Thrusting faster, the leather strap of the harness pulling and pressing hard against her slit, groaning as the womon dug her nails into her flesh, Tita came.

Tita kissed the womon gently as the womon wrapped her arms around Tita, holding her close. The two wimmin lay together that way as their pounding hearts slowed.
Finally, Tita got up and lit them fresh cigarettes. They finished their drinks in silence and then got dressed.

λ λ λ

The parking lot was almost empty when the two finally emerged from the van. Tita walked the womon to her car.
Unlocking the door, the womon turned to Tita and kissed her lightly on the lips. "That was incredible, honey. I think this one's my favorite."
Tita watched the womon climb into the car and turn the ignition. Lowering the window the womon said, "So I'll see you back home in a few minutes?"
Tita smiled warmly and touched her partner's cheek. "I'm right behind you, baby."

AUTUMN

It's raining and cold today. Even sitting near this roaring fire, I am chilly. I miss your arms, your body.

When was the last time you were here? It seems so long ago—a Hallowe'en though—I remember because we carved a jack-o-lantern and made love by its light.

You were sitting on the floor, a quilt wrapped around your naked body. I brought in cups of hot cider and you welcomed me into your cocoon. We sat together, silent, smelling the cinnamon from our cups and the spicy pumpkin roasting by candle flame in the window.

In that dim light, I could just make out the details of your face—years of care and worry, joy and pain etched between your brows and at the corners of your mouth.

I kissed you, tasting rum and apples on your tongue. You held me close, breast to breast. I could feel your heart beating against me.

You cupped my face between your hands and kissed my eyes, my nose, my chin. My lips begged you to touch them, but you ignored their cry, kissing my neck and shoulders, the swell of my breasts. My nipples grew erect under your tender attentions. Each time you suckled me, currents of electricity jolted through my body, going to my center—my womonhood—it pulsated with your power.

I gripped you to me, pulling you up, up to my lips and as we kissed, we sank back—me to the floor, you to my arms. Moving together, thigh to thigh, belly to belly, we moved in the ancient dance of the Temples—giving and receiving the Pleasures of the Mother.

As the candle melted, the wax dripping out and on to the table, so too I melted, my liquid self pouring out on the carpet beneath me.

I felt you too—your breath hot, ragged as you whispered incantations in my ear, hypnotizing me, anointing me with your oils. I became your priestess, your supplicant tending your shrine. I tasted your plump, ripe fruit and drank your sacred wine—and you came—and lifted me to the heavens with you.

How can I bear Autumn without you? I miss you. I wish you were here.

THE PAINTER

I was an art major at a well known university in New England when I met Phoebe. A star in the department by my junior year, I had already done two shows receiving enthusiastic reviews. I didn't date or go out with friends on the weekend. My only passion was developing and perfecting my craft.

It was late September and the days were still warm, though winter whispered its arrival on breezes that blew the colorful leaves from the trees. I was working on a new piece for my first one-woman show and spent every afternoon in a spare studio in the department.

That's where I was when Phoebe slipped into my life. Oh, she wasn't a complete stranger. She was in my Tuesday and Thursday mornings sculpting class, and though we had never spoken, I had noticed her. It would have been impossible not to.

Phoebe was tall, almost six feet. At twenty-four, her hair, curly and worn closely cropped to her perfect skull, was already salt and pepper. Her body was toned, like a dancer's, with small breasts over a tight, flat stomach. Her legs, long and slender, curved gracefully into a firm, lusciously rounded ass.

"I didn't know anyone else was up here. I'm next door working." She walked over to my easel and stood next to me. I could smell the slightly spicy scent she wore, mixed with sweat and the earthy smell of the clay she worked with. My mouth watered. She was talking.

"I've seen some of your oils and I'm a big admirer. I just can't seem to find a voice in that medium. Would you mind if I watched you work for a few minutes?"

She didn't wait for an answer, but turned and walked to the exhibit table behind me. As she moved across the room, I couldn't help but compare her body to mine, because we so contrasted physically. I too was tall, about five-foot-nine, but I had a softer body, large breasts, rounded hips and thighs. My hair, despite all efforts to control it, remained a frizzy mane of shoulder length auburn. Where Phoebe's skin was dark and flawless, mine was light and heavily freckled.

Forcing myself to concentrate on the canvas, I picked up my palette and continued working. Phoebe sat on the table behind me and watched me paint.

The room was cool and quiet, save the scraping of the paint knife as I mixed colors. I could feel Phoebe's presence behind me, her black eyes studying me. She stayed for about ten minutes and then, without a goodbye, slipped out of the room.

She started dropping by in the afternoons to watch me paint. Occasionally she would ask questions about technique, but mostly she sat quietly with her sketch pad and worked. She didn't ask personal questions, never tried to push the tentative friendship we seemed to be forging. I had always been so absorbed in my work that I had never bothered making friends on campus, and I was surprised to find that it felt good to have someone around. In fact, it was I who suggested coffee one night after I'd pulled the cloth over my canvas.

We began to spend time together. I was very comfortable talking with Phoebe. Her deep voice soothed and excited me at the same time. My nights began to be filled with fantasies of her. I felt a strange tingling down my spine, moistness between my legs whenever I recalled the way she moved, the way she sat on the work table under the window. When I closed my eyes I would recall her scent, could almost feel her skin against mine, her hands caressing my body, her legs wrapped around me, pulling me closer. . . .

I didn't know what was happening to me. Seeing the autumn sun reflecting on Phoebe's swarthy skin, I added golden tones to my picture. I imagined myself falling into her dark eyes, saw myself exploring the mystery of her murky depths, and added those mists and shadows to my canvas. My professor commented on the richer, deeper expression in my work and encouraged me to explore this new direction more fully.

I never said a word about my growing feelings to Phoebe. I didn't know how she would take hearing another woman say that she loved her. But I also had a selfish reason. I was almost finished with my painting. I just couldn't risk losing her or the secret passion that was fueling what was no doubt my best work ever.

And too, I didn't know how to approach the subject. How could I convey my feelings in a way she might accept? I expressed myself with oils, not words. How could I tell her how she made me feel? Afternoon shadows were falling across the room and I was putting the final touches on my painting. I stood back a little, examining my work, when Phoebe slipped quietly in behind me. She studied the canvas for a moment, a bare smile playing at the corners of her mouth. She turned to me then, a look of surprise and, and something else. Suddenly embarrassed, I turned abruptly back to the easel. Phoebe stepped away, I thought to the table, though I couldn't look up after her, lest I give myself away. Dabbing color here and there, my heart pounding, I tried to calm myself.

And then Phoebe was behind me again. I could hear her breathing, feel her warm breath on my cheek. She just had coffee, I thought wildly to myself as she took the brush from my hand, placing it in the can of turpentine on the stool beside me.

She reached beneath my sweater. Goosebumps rose on my arms as she gently stroked my breasts. My nipples hardened in her palm, and then she gathered my top in her hands and pulled it over my head. I closed my eyes as she pressed against me and lightly kissed my shoulders. My heart fluttered and I felt a gush of hot wetness pool between my thighs when I leaned back into her and discovered she was naked.

Phoebe unzipped my jeans and worked them down. Now we were both standing naked, exposed to the golden light of the fading day.

Phoebe guided me to the table. Her hands were gentle, firm. She molded my body like the clay she sculpted. Her kisses were deep, her tongue probing, soft. I couldn't believe what was happening. My fantasy was becoming reality and I suddenly didn't know what to do. I shyly reached out to her and Phoebe smiled as she guided my hand downward, to her damp pussy.

I touched my fingers to my lips, tentatively tasting the creamy wetness I found curled in the hairs between Phoebe's legs. Finding it pleasurable, I looked into her eyes and, seeing her acquiescence, slid down her body, searching for its source.

I took in her scent, heightened by her excitement, and then kissed her mound, wetting my face in her juicy abundance. I licked her lips, her softer inner lips, and flicked my tongue over her hooded button. She pressed herself down on my face, and I gasped at the shock of exhilaration that coursed through me. Hungrily, I thrust my tongue in and out of her pulsating hole.

Phoebe held my head closer to her as I flicked over her hard, swollen clit. She gyrated her body slowly, teaching my mouth how to love her the way she liked. My own pussy was throbbing, soaking the papers beneath me, and I began to finger myself frantically.

Phoebe's breathing was getting harsher, her body tensing. She was playing with her breasts, squeezing and pinching the nipples as her excitement grew. She was gasping, "Yes, baby, yes. Suck it just like that. Harder, ooh baby, I'm cumming, yes, yesssssss!"

Her body arched in orgasm and she drenched my face in wave after wave of her delicious cream.

Phoebe pulled me up and rolled me beneath her. We kissed deeply, her hands caught in my tangle of hair. Tugging my head back, Phoebe caught a bit of tender throat in her mouth and then released it. She was biting me lightly on my neck, my shoulders, my breasts. Reaching for my wrists, she held them above my head and began flicking her tongue over the sparse hairs under my arms, smiling slightly as a low moan escaped my lips.

Phoebe teased me with her mouth, her hands, her body, leaving no place untouched. Each time I neared orgasm, Phoebe would back off until I was begging her to be released. I couldn't believe how hot I was. I thrust my hips up and out—inviting—imploring her to enter, but Phoebe just continued her search of all the secret, sensitive places on my body.

I had never felt like this before. "Please. Oh god, please!" I whimpered. I needed to cum so badly. And then Phoebe raised herself above me, and looking me in the eyes, pushed one finger into me. I arched my back, taking it, wanting more. Two fingers, then three. I consumed them, hungered for them. I clamped my muscled walls down and brazenly rode Phoebe's hand.

Grinding my cunt into her hand, an orgasm quickly building again, I grabbed Phoebe's wrist, urging her to pump harder, faster. I cried out, "please, please don't stop."

Phoebe was talking to me, low and harsh, "You want it, baby? You want me to give it to you? Come on, baby, let it go, that's right. . . ." I couldn't take it, I couldn't hold on any longer. And when Phoebe pressed her thumb into my clit, I screamed, cumming so hard that my body shook helplessly.

Phoebe wrapped her arms around me until I calmed down. I couldn't believe I was crying, the experience so overwhelming.

I know it's a cliché, but yes—soon thereafter I packed my bags and moved in with her. We lived together for the remainder of our undergraduate careers, and then, picking the same masters program, we moved down to the Sunshine State.

Well, it's been twelve years since that late autumn afternoon, and we are still together. We live in a beautiful beach house in southern Florida. Phoebe went on to get her doctorate and is an art professor at a university here. I work full time with my oils and have established quite a reputation in the art world.

Making love is still as exciting as it was when we first met, but there is so much more to our relationship than the physical. Our love is intense, nurturing, healing. Phoebe fertilizes the soil of my creativity with her passions. She tells me that my love renews her spirit.

There have been many lucrative offers over the years for the oil I was working on when we met, but of course I could never sell it. The painting is proudly and prominently displayed in our home, its brilliant colors, its dusky shadows, a reminder of love—set aflame on a New England autumn afternoon.

THE SPA

You say you need to get away? Relax? Going through a stack of brochures but can't find a place that "resonates"? Have you considered North Carolina? No? Well, after you've heard my story, you may want to reconsider. You won't get a recommendation like this from any travel agent.

I am an attractive and healthy, 34-year-old African-American lesbian, living in Harlem. I own a small but very profitable computer consulting business with offices in midtown Manhattan. Now there are many advantages to being an entrepreneur, my favorite being that I am under no pressure to conform to heterosexist "norms." Databases are not homophobic.

But there is also tremendous responsibility in running a business. Making payroll, finding new clients and nurturing old ones, rent, electricity, insurance—get the picture? Well, usually I can take the vicissitudes of this life in stride, but the last fiscal quarter had been a bitch, leaving me edgy and snappish. A friend had sent over a vacation catalog that

I had tossed into a mound of junk mail on my secretary's desk. It reappeared mysteriously one morning on my chair, a yellow stick-em marking a page describing an "ultra pampering spa" and a typewritten note saying "PLEASE do it."

I knew I really needed to get away for a few days, but there were deadlines to meet, demos to schedule, clients to soothe—we were overbooked and understaffed—a pleasant headache—but a headache nonetheless.

My secretary, Toni, came in with the morning mail and caught me eyeing the brochure. "Taking a vacation?" She asked, rather too hopefully, I thought.

"No. Just fantasizing. There's too much going on right now for a vacation." I tossed the magazine aside.

Toni, bless her brave heart, pressed on. "You know, a vacation is probably just what we—I mean *you* need. I'm sure we can hold down the fort for a few days. I could reschedule your appointments from Wednesday on and have tickets delivered today. What do you say?"

"Are you trying to get rid of me?" I rubbed my eyes and continued briskly, "Give me the mail and get ITC on the line."

Toni turned to leave. "And, Toni? I'll consider it."

Well, all morning my staff stopped by, friendly, concerned, assuring me they would *reluctantly* do without me for a few days. I called Toni in to make the arrangements, and she had the tickets and itinerary in her hands already. Wishful thinking?

The staff practically shoved me out of the office that Tuesday afternoon, sending me off to the airport and a six-day spa getaway in the mountains of North Carolina.

There was a storm warning in effect over the tri-state area all day, but the first flurries hit the windshield of my cab as we headed over the Triborough Bridge.

We were delayed in the terminal for over an hour before being allowed to board, only to be held on the runway another two hours before being cleared for take off. The attendants offered alcoholic compensation, but they didn't have enough liquor on board to even begin to put a dent in my tension—so I didn't even start.

To compound my misery, the plane was packed, and I was seated beside a womon and her three-year-old terror. When we touched down in Charlotte, I knew every goddamned word to the "Barney" song, and I had a bitching headache. That's the space I was in when I arrived at the spa.

Fortunately, they had had the foresight to have a massage scheduled immediately after registration. I dropped my bags in a comfortable, well-appointed room, and followed a staffer to the massage center where, snatching a towel from her impatiently, I quickly stripped and went to my assigned room.

It was painted a subtle blue, the bare walls broken by a single window looking out on the tennis courts, now stripped of nets and covered with a layer of frost that concealed the green clay beneath. There was a cart in one corner, crowded with oils, sponges, spray bottles and stuff, a chair near the door, and a table in the center of the room, pillow and sheet crisp and white. I lay on the table, crossed my arms under my head and closed my eyes. I tried to breathe deeply, willing myself to relax, exhaling the stale air of New York City, the tensions of my flight. A knock on the door. I opened my eyes as a stunning womon peeked in. "Ready?" she asked in a husky, slightly accented voice.

For what, I wondered as I nodded her in. I watched her drop her bag and begin preparations. I was feeling better already. About five-foot-six, she was trim and buffed. I could see the sinewy muscles move even under her uniform of white polo and sweats. Her hair, black and wavy, was tied back in a ponytail, with wisps playing about her ears and—gorgeous neck. Her almond-shaped eyes were as deep and as ancient green as the Central American rain forests of her ancestors.

I watched her move efficiently about the small room, lighting a candle under a pot of herbs, pressing a button on a small recorder, which instantly filled the room with the soothing strains of Native American flute. I was liking this, okay?

Finally, she turned to me, and her mauve-colored lips parted, revealing a charming chipped front tooth in an otherwise flawless smile.

"I will start with an overall massage, and then work any areas giving you problems?" She ended the sentence in a question I don't think she *really* wanted me to respond to.

Her touch was firm, gentle, professional. She molded and squeezed my thighs, calves; she rubbed my ass and pummeled my shoulders. She ordered me on my back and worked my neck, breasts, stomach, she pulled and pushed apart my thighs and I wished, I dreaded, that her hands would brush my dampening pussy. If she noticed my discomfiture, she gave no indication.

Completing the job she said, "I'll leave you to rest for a few minutes. Take your time. Please give this voucher to the front desk when you leave the center." And she was gone.

I lay there, feeling surprisingly contented and relaxed, listening to people talking in the hallway, the faint clanging of free weights, a wind picking up outside. Then, sitting up, I reached over and picked up the slip she had left me. "One massage. Marisol."

λ λ λ

Over the next couple of days I got into the spa rhythm, spending a lot of time catching up on my recreational reading from the comfort of the poolside Jacuzzi. I would position myself, from time to time, in front of the jets and watch Marisol go about her work, as the streaming water titillated my pussy. She would occasionally glance my way and smile, but she didn't give me any more energy than that. I had two more massages, after that first, and though the wimmin were proficient, they weren't Marisol.

You know, I was a little peeved. I mean, we *were* the only sisters there, and for no other reason than that, I'd have thought she'd be more friendly. Well, the hell with her then, I thought to myself as I sipped my water with lemon ice cubes.

Getting out of the whirlpool, I wrapped a towel around my waist and consulted my itinerary. Salt scrub in one hour. Good, I had time. Padding over to the phone, I placed a long distance call, setting up a date on the night of my return home. Shit. It's not like I was *starving*.

Marisol was walking toward me, arms full of towels. She wasn't really my type anyway.

"I see you have a salt scrub scheduled. That's with me. Why don't you spend a few minutes in the sauna and then take a shower in stall three. I'm going to leave a loofah and special cleanser for you. Wash up and I'll meet you in Room C in . . ." she looked across the room at the big clock, "say forty-five minutes?" Then she passed me, bumping the swing doors open with her—yes, it really was—fine ass and disappearing into the dressing rooms.

Well, I could be "that way" too, I sniffed. After all, she *was* just an employee—here to make my life pleasant. I didn't need to be more familiar with the help anyway.

I left my suit on the hook outside the sauna and stepped into the hot, dry cubicle. I found a small bucket of eucalyptus water, a spray bottle, and a bowl with two quartered oranges set up on the lower bench. As the gym was practically deserted at this time of day, I assumed they were left for me. I poured the scented liquid over the coals and climbed to the upper level as the water hissed and popped. I lay back, breathing in the burning air slowly, and sprayed my body with the icy spritzer. Then I peeled a section of orange and stuffed it into my mouth, savoring its sweet, tangy juice as it dripped down my throat. Life was good.

Eventually, I remembered my appointment and headed for the showers. As promised, a sponge, covered with a green substance, awaited me. Feeling pampered and satisfied, I padded to Room C.

Marisol was waiting for me, the room already prepared. Imperiously, I dropped my towel on the floor, smiling childishly to myself as I watched her bend to retrieve it. She folded it neatly and put it on the chair as I lay, face down, on the table.

"Turn over please." Marisol commanded. "I am going to start with a light, invigorating rubdown with this marine spray, then follow with progressively more abrasive salt mixtures. After you rinse off again, I will finish with a massage with essential oils."

"Whatever." I thought to myself as I closed my eyes. Marisol took a bottle from the cart and sprayed a light, cool mist over my body. I could smell the ocean—pungent, fishy, and fresh all at once.

She drummed her fingers rapidly over my skin and then began squeezing my muscles between her fingers. She started talking as she worked.

"Have you been enjoying your stay?" she pulled and twisted my neck.

"Ummm. It's been relaxing. I really needed this."

She pummeled my shoulders. "Do you generally take vacations without your—spouse?"

I smiled. "I'm single."

She was massaging my breasts, talking casually, "I can't believe that a womon as attractive as you are doesn't have a man." Her fingers brushed my hardening nipples.

"I don't date men."

Her hands hesitated for a moment and then continued to rub my belly in a slow, circular motion. "And it doesn't bother you—being alone?"

She was working my thighs, kneading them firmly. "Please open your legs a little." Her voice was getting thick. There were tiny beads of sweat on her upper lip.

"I never said I was alone. I said I don't date men."

Marisol's knuckle brushed my mound. She was working my upper, inner thighs, breathing deeply.

I could see her nipples, hard, pushing against the fabric of her shirt. I wondered what color they were.

"So you . . . um . . . you don't go out with men?" she asked me, face inscrutable as she finished off my calves and began massaging my feet. She pressed them against her (crotch?—I couldn't see—only hope) as she manipulated each toe and then flexed my feet. "Please turn over."

I rolled on my stomach, pussy throbbing. Was I reading into things, or was she getting turned on too?

"Yes, I am a lesbian. That *is* what you're trying to ask?"

Her hands were purposely lingering on my ass. I was sure of it. I felt myself dripping on the sheet beneath me. I hoped that Marisol couldn't smell my arousal.

"You know, I was surprised when I saw you that first day. You're the first womon of color I've seen up here since I started. I can't tell you how lonely it gets sometimes."

Marisol's hand slipped between my thighs, her finger playing along my soaking slit. "Ahhh," she breathed.

I closed my eyes, shifting my legs open wider. "You . . . you don't have a lover?" My voice was shaking.

Exploring my swelling inner folds, she whispered, "My lover stayed on in Atlanta. We haven't broken up officially, but I haven't seen her in almost five months." Her finger dipped into my hole. My body contracted.

She slipped another finger in and twisted her wrist so that her thumb pressed against my clit as I bore down and ground it. I moaned.

"*Ay dios mio.* It seems like forever since I've touched a womon. You are *muy rica*—so delicious." Her fingers slowly pumped me.

Her other hand squeezed my ass, and then I felt her lips pressed against that plump, sensitive mound. Her hands pushed my legs further apart and I felt her tongue flickering around my pussy, now stuffed with three fingers, twisting, pushing me slowly up the incline toward orgasm.

She lapped at me feverishly, up and down the crack of my ass, then rimmed me. The sensation of thumb thrumming, fingers pumping, tongue rimming—GODDESS! I came.

She collapsed on my back, breathing heavily, kissing my shoulder blades. "You are so sweet—so sweet." She murmured over and over.

There was a knock on the door. Marisol stood abruptly and, picking up a towel to wipe her face, opened the door slightly.

I could hear someone apologizing for interrupting, and then reminding her that she was running late—I couldn't make out the rest. "Okay, thanks Lisa." Marisol closed the door and turned to me.

"I have another appointment in ten minutes. Would you like to continue this 'session' later this evening—say after the gym closes at 8:30?"

I sat up, swinging my legs to the floor. "Where shall we meet—my room?"

Marisol shook her head. "Staff is not allowed to fraternize with the guests. In fact, only housekeeping is allowed on the guest floors. Why don't you come here—around 8:20ish. Hang out in the steam room and once I've let the staff out and locked up, I'll meet you there. Okay?"

"I'll see you tonight," I promised.

She winked at me and slipped out.

λ λ λ

I was so excited at the prospect of a clandestine rendezvous that I overdid it at the gym. I mean I worked out on the weights and treadmill; I sweated on the bikes and Stairmaster. I limped into the dining area at dinner and sat down wearily. The other guests were making plans to see a movie and invited me to join them. I begged off, pleading sore muscles (and throbbing pussy—though I didn't mention that part). Someone suggested I run back over to the gym and spend a few quiet moments in the Jacuzzi before turning in early. I thanked them for their suggestion and concern—and then ran like the dickens to keep my appointment.

λ λ λ

Once you get used to the hot, moist air, the steam room is really relaxing. I spread my towel out and lay down. I love the thrill of anticipation—but I really had worked my body earlier in the afternoon. Despite my excitement, my body got heavier and heavier, and I dozed off.

I dreamed I was standing in the Amazon jungles. There was something coming at me through the mist-shrouded greenery. My heart was pounding—I couldn't move or see. Suddenly the mist parted and I saw Marisol.

"Are you awake?" She knelt, naked, beside me. I reached out and touched her face. "Marisol?"

"Come on." She pulled me up and led me to the door, but then stopped and turned to me. "Stand right here." She positioned me beside her and then pulled a chain I hadn't noticed before.

I screamed as cold water showered down over me. She laughed and joined me under the icy torrent. Pulling my face down to hers, she kissed me passionately, pressing her lithe body against mine.

She was hungry. That always really turns me on. We backed over to my towel and I sat her down. Then I knelt between her parted thighs. Realizing my intent, she leaned back, resting her head on the wall, opening her thighs further.

I leaned into her pussy, smelling her essence. I rubbed my face in her thicket, my tongue and nose dipping into her syrupy opening.

She sighed, her muscles relaxing as she let me take control. I started slowly, containing my own excitement so I could feel out her pleasure. I ran my tongue slowly up and down her glossy cavern, stopping to tug ever so gently on her distended hood.

Her body quivered. God she was hot! I wanted to give her a slow, lingering experience, so I reluctantly left that tasty bud and continued up her body. Her hands played in my hair, guiding me with gentle pressure to her sensitive places.

Marisol loved having her breasts sucked. I locked my mouth on her soft, plump mounds and alternatively rolled and tugged her deep rose nipples with my tongue and teeth. At the same time, I teased her dripping cunt with my hand. The steam and our passion glistened on her, highlighting the rippling muscles of her thighs, her stomach tense, even as her insides pulsed around my fingers in orgasm.

She pulled me up from the floor and kissed me hard. "Let's take a swim!" She bolted from the room.

I followed her.

She dove into the water, swimming strong strokes to the deep end of the pool. She turned to me, smiling. "Can you swim?"

"Like a shark!" I answered as I jumped in. The cool water felt good on my skin after the heat of the steam room. I swam the length of the pool underwater, coming up for a big gulp of air when I saw Marisol's legs a few feet from me. I sucked her pussy with the last of my breath.

We lounged at the edge of the pool for a little while, talking, laughing, trailing fingers and lips on each other's bodies until we were panting. She looked at me—eyes serious. "Let's go back to Room C and finish your session there."

λ λ λ

There were scented candles burning in hand-painted bowls. Fresh rose petals floated in the water of those bowls, and I could smell sandlewood and vanilla mixing with that floral scent.

Marisol closed the door behind us and I stepped toward her, but she stopped me, holding up her hand.

"No. Up on the table. Face up." Her voice was low, thick. We weren't playing any more.

Who was I to argue? I climbed on the table as commanded, and she reached for her gym bag, which was sitting on the stool near the door. Then she pulled the cart closer and hung her bag on its edge.

"What are you going to. . . ."

"Shhhh. Just relax. You *did* request an aroma therapy massage, yes? It's on your schedule."

Marisol picked up a bottle and poured a generous amount of its liquid into her hand. Rubbing her palms together briskly to warm the oil, Marisol then placed her hot, healing hands upon me.

Her strong, steady strokes were professional—except that as she worked my shoulders and down my arm, her lips would, from time to time, follow her fingers. And when she reached my hand, she tongued my palm and lasciviously sucked my fingers and the valleys between them.

My clit was pumping so hard, my whole pelvis lifted off the table in response. I groaned as her lips released my hand and she continued the erotic moldings of my flesh.

My body rocked and bucked as she played with my aching pussy.

"Oooh, baby," she crooned as her hand slipped in and out of me. "I think you're ready for more."

Without removing the hand working me, Marisol reached into her bag and pulled out a thick, double-headed dildo.

Now I had never really gone for that sort of thing, but Marisol had one end of it sliding in and out of her juicy hole while she played with my pussy—and she could do any damn thing she wanted to me.

She was concentrating, her nostrils flaring, as she rode that rod in rhythm with her pumping hand in me.

Her body was quaking, shivering, as she struggled to maintain control. Climbing up on the table, she urged my legs over her shoulders and pushed the other end of that dildo into me. Then she slid her steaming box down—down until her cavern was filled and we rode her toy, humping pussy to pounding pussy.

Marisol grunted and moaned, eyes squeezed shut as she focused on the feelings she was invoking.

I thought she had left me to enter her own world of fantasy, but she opened her eyes, the pupils so dilated they looked black. Then she arched her back until her tits pointed to the sky. Hot damn! I threw my legs over the sides of the table so she could get closer, deeper inside me.

She reached into her gym bag again, and this time pulled out a small vibrator. She turned it on and put it lightly but directly on my engorged sex.

I reached up, grabbing her by her nipples and pulling her down to me so that the vibrator was wedged between us.

I gave myself over to our lust and shamelessly came—wrapping my legs around her waist, gripping her ass as she surrendered to her volcano's eruption.

It was almost 4:30 a.m. before I returned, weak and bowlegged back to my room.

I believe we left a bit of—color—in every room and on every piece of equipment in that gym in the ensuing nights before I returned to New York—relaxed, toned, *and* tuned up (fer shurr).

We exchanged cards and "if-you're-evers" the night before I left. My last memory of the spa was Marisol, smiling and waving as my cab headed down the driveway to the airport.

λ λ λ

It's amazing how a little vacation can put a new blush on your life. Business has been good these past few months. I've taken on new clients and expanded my office, adding two new account managers and another secretary. I've decided to reward my success with a trip somewhere.

Now let's see—where might a hard working executive go for a bit of relaxation and pampering?

I've heard tell of a little spa in the mountains of North Carolina....

APPETIZERS

Carmen opened her eyes and waited for them to adjust to the darkness. It was almost 9:00 p.m. and she was famished. Paula lay sleeping beside her, one arm thrown over her head, red hair short and fuzzy except for a long tail that now draped over her shoulder, tickling a mauve-colored nipple that peeked out of the opening of her robe. Carmen held her breath and carefully undid the tie, watching in pleasure as Paula's beautiful body was exposed.

Paula's skin, smooth, heavily freckled and richly caramel-colored, flowed over her rounded, ring-pierced belly and melted into the neatly trimmed triangle of red-blonde pubic hair. Carmen ran her hand lightly over Paula's rippling thighs and felt a low throbbing as she envisioned herself trapped between them.

As she softly kissed each small, thrusting breast, Carmen felt herself growing wet. She moved her hand down to her moistening clef, wishing her flicking finger was Paula's tongue on her sensitive button. Electric shocks surged through her and she pressed harder, rubbed faster as her excitement built. Trying not to awaken Paula, but urgently needing to get off, Carmen lay back, closing her eyes, and imagined the taste of Paula's juices on her lips, the saltiness of Paula's sweaty skin as they made love. Her pulse was quickening when, without warning, Paula's mouth was on her.

Paula ran her tongue along the inner rim of Carmen's lips, sucking on Carmen's swollen clit and as Carmen exploded, her orgasm shooting through her, Carmen's body was forced up in a spasm of ecstasy. Her body trembled as Paula softly licked her, bringing her back, smearing her face with Carmen's abundant wetness.

Moving up, Paula kissed her passionately, her now salty tongue seeking Carmen's. And then Carmen rolled Paula over and began kissing Paula down her spine and up again. Her breath was on Paula's neck, in her ear, feverishly telling Paula how hot she was, how hard she was going to make Paula cum as she humped Paula's ass.

Carmen's juices dripped into Paula's steaming crack, mixing with Paula's cream in a pool beneath them.

She reached hungrily between Paula's legs, the weight of both bodies pressing Paula's wet, pulsating pussy down on Carmen's strong hands. Paula's soprano cry joined with Carmen's contralto moan in sweet harmony as they came.

They lay there, bodies tangled in the damp sheets. Somewhere a radio was turned up, and salsa penetrated the quiet of the room. Suddenly Carmen's stomach gave a loud grumble and they both burst out laughing.

"Well," Paula gasped, "I guess I was just an appetizer. Fine. We'll go have a *real* meal now."

THE FESTIVAL

I was excited. Not just because it was my first wimmin's music festival, but because it was the first Wimmin of Color festival, and heading up security, I was waist deep in a rainbow river of golden hues, surrounded by the arms and smiles and energies of my sisters. I floated on a cloud of patchouli and sage, as the wimmin registered, set up camp, and commenced the making of history.

I stood in the Commons, walkie-talkie in one hand, giving directions with the other, wishing I'd had the foresight to have grown a third so I could relieve my aroused condition, which grew more intense each time a gap-toothed woman in khakis and t-shirt, or queen with flowing locks and ankle bells, or shaved-headed sister with nose ring and combat boots, offered me a warm embrace of welcome.

It was a glorious day.

I had heard that wimmin's festivals were the perfect environments for letting go of inhibitions, getting in touch with one's physical and spiritual selves, reclaiming one's primal voice and connectedness with the Mother.

Okay. But I wanted to meet wimmin.

Now don't misunderstand: all of those things I just mentioned were important to me, but I am an attractive, single, healthy, and energetic lesbian. I have very few single friends, and those single wimmin I do have acquaintance with—well, let's just say, I don't want them "that way." I figured that, amidst all this spirituality, I might find someone to connect with on a more—earthly plane.

But I was determined not to obsess—in fact, I wasn't going to have a moment to ponder the possibilities any more that day as I dashed from sight to sight. Every time I stopped to speak to someone for more than a minute, I was hailed on my radio and off I'd have to run.

The first night, everyone gathered for the opening ceremony. Everyone but me, that is. Wimmin were still arriving and I was trapped in the security building registering and finding space for tired travelers. It was 2:30 a.m. before I finally climbed under my blanket (alone) to sleep.

The next morning we held a welcome and orientation session after breakfast. As I waited for my turn at the mike, I scanned the room full of wimmin, smiling acknowledgment to familiar faces. Almost directly across from me, a womon, draped in brightly colored fabrics, studied me. I caught her eye, but her gaze didn't waver. I blushed at her boldness, quickly averting my eyes and stumbling forward as my name was called.

You had to see it. Walkie-talkie secured to my belted drummer pants; a scanty half-shirt barely concealing my ample breasts; long, dangling earrings; and yes—makeup. I stood, legs apart, in complete control—the femme commando. I started running down festival safety do's and don'ts, when I was summoned on my radio. (Perfect timing!) With a few parting words to the wimmin and (I hoped) a dashing smile, Super Femme flew from the room to right wrongs and save the Festival.

Well, *that* novelty wore off as quickly as the day progressed. Everyone seemed to be enjoying themselves—making friends, attending workshops, sitting, breasts bared, on the green hills around the day stage. I watched wistfully, resentfully, as I answered yet another distress call.

Just after lunch, the womon I had seen studying me earlier asked if I could help her put up her tent. "You said to just grab you," she laughed as she pulled me along.

She was breathtaking, dressed in an emerald green robe, her dark auburn, waist-length locks decorated with cowry shells, engraved silver cuffs, and other ornaments. An assortment of earrings dangled from her ears, which were pierced from rim to lobe, and she wore a thin gold hoop in her nose.

I watched her float down the path before me. She was stunning—but not my type—I mean, I had never dated what I call the "lock crowd," mostly because I couldn't clearly tell who was femme or butch and that confused and disconcerted me. As far as I could tell she was femme, and I wasn't into femmes. I don't mind topping from time to time—but . . . so I just enjoyed her beauty and left it at that.

Anyway, I helped her move from the cabins to the tent village, and in the process we got to talking. There was something about Raina—that's her name—that I found soothing and comfortable. Our conversation flowed effortlessly over a wide range of subjects. As we sat in the grass in front of her tent, I watched her gazing skyward as she sought words to color the image she was at that moment creating for me. Suddenly, I had the urge to kiss her. She was saying something to me. Her lips moving, her tongue slipping between her teeth—I was sure she was talking—but I couldn't hear her. I was consumed with a desire to taste her—her skin, lips—I leaned toward her and her mouth went still, anticipating. Our lips touched gently, sweetly. I could smell citrus and earth.

My walkie-talkie crackled to life, breaking the spell. An emergency at security. I jumped up, brushing grass. "I'm sorry. On my way—out."

Raina smiled. "It's okay. I'll see you later."

But later didn't come. The shuttle driver had disappeared, and there were people at the station. I was the only other person insured to drive the van. On the way back from town, the van broke down and by the time I got back—well, it was after 11:00 p.m. before I was able to sit at my desk and pick at the cold dinner a staff member had thoughtfully procured for me.

A late night arrival damaged one of the parked cars, and the next morning was spent sorting out that mess. I missed breakfast—again, I had had only three hours of sleep—again. It was the last full day of the festival, and I hadn't had a single hot meal or seen any of the performances. I was pissed, okay? So when the accident was resolved, I stomped up to the office and slammed the door to my room—determined to take a nap.

The walkie-talkie crackled "Emergency in parking—please come down immediately—out."

"Goddamn it! Can't you handle it? I'm busy—out."

"No. I don't know what to do, and I'm the only one down here. My relief didn't show up—out."

Shit. "Okay. On my way—out." Why had I volunteered? Where the hell was everyone else? Can't depend on anyone—have to do everything myself. I cursed and muttered as I made my way down the path, passing wimmin holding hands, talking, laughing. Glad *they* were having a good time.

"What's the problem?" I growled at my friend, who sat on the bench in the quiet registration area, sipping a soda and nonchalantly reading a book—her walkie-talkie on the table beside her.

"I don't know. Some kind of racket down there." She nodded casually toward the unoccupied cabins on the other side of the unmown field.

"And you had to call me? You couldn't check it out yourself?" I shouted.

"I'm from Brooklyn. I don't walk in anybody's grass if I can't see the ground. Something might bite me."

I wanted to slap her. Instead, I turned my back to her, looking across the field, trying to maintain some calm.

Raina was standing at the entrance to one of the cabins, smiling. I turned back to my friend who winked at me. I nudged her shoulder and then headed into the tall grass.

"This was the only way I could think of to get a few minutes of your time." She reached for my hand and pulled me into the coolness of the wooden shelter.

One of the bunks had a sleeping bag on it. This Raina sat on, patting the space beside her.

I sat beside her, suddenly nervous. I couldn't look at her. I listened to the sounds of nature—bees hovering around a hive in the rafters outside the screened windows, birds calling to one another, Raina breathing.

She touched my thigh. "This hasn't been much of a festival for you?" Her long fingers squeezed my flesh between them.

"I'm tired, hungry.... I haven't been able to sit for a minute. The first wimmin of color festival—everyone else looks so happy—like they've made friends and I haven't had time to meet anyone." A petulant note of self pity had found its way into my voice. Yuk.

"Now is that *really* true? You haven't made *any* new friends?" She smiled, indulging the brat, even as she traced a pattern up my thigh, my arm, before lifting my chin until I looked into her eyes.

She kissed me. Goddess! My entire body jumped in response as she pulled me closer, as she kissed me more insistently—as I returned her intensity. Her hand moved behind my neck, stroking the little hairs there, pulling on my ear with her teeth. I was dizzy—would have fallen had I been standing. I was weak, hypnotized as she guided me back on the sleeping bag and lay beside me, one leg thrown between mine, pressing me down, and closer to her.

My hands found their way beneath her robes to the satiny skin beneath, as her mouth traced down my neck and across the hollow of my shoulder.

I shifted my body for closer contact, as her thigh pressed more firmly against my crotch. I moaned—wet, throbbing—and with a burst of strength I pulled her fully on me. We began to grind, slowly, in rhythm with our tongues, our hearts. Her skin was damp, my fingers running rivers down her spine. She was naked beneath her robes—had I mentioned that?

I fingered the beads she wore around her hips, clutched her ass closer to me and arched my back as her hand slipped beneath me. Our movements deepened, synchronized. I felt that wonderful tingling sensation beginning.

Raina's eyes were closed, brow furrowed, beads of sweat across her freckled nose. She bit her lower lip in concentration of passion growing.

I felt my own tides rising, my body stiffening with the tension of anticipated release. I held my breath, digging in deeper, riding harder.

There was a sudden blast of horns moments before the sound of metal connecting, the strident tones of angry voices.

"Get out here, oh shit! Hurry up!"

I'd be lying if I didn't say I'd hoped—at least for a minute (or two)—that someone was dead—as Raina, sighing with frustration rolled off the bunk, adjusting her robes.

"You're the only one who knows CPR and first aid, I suppose?" she said wryly as she watched me smooth down my rumpled top.

"I'm . . ."

"Yeah, I know. Sorry . . . and responsible and, and, and. Just go on. Duty calls."

"I'm on my way—out." With great reluctance and regret, I pushed open the cabin door and jogged across the field.

The accident was minor. Someone else could have handled it. That's all I'm going to say about that.

λ λ λ

Lights were on in some of the cabins. Jackets were thrown over shoulders. The air was cooling, the day turning to night. The final evening of the festival people would talk about for years to come, and I had missed it. I'd even lost my chance with Raina.

After the scene in the cabin was interrupted, I had decided that I would take the rest of the afternoon off no matter what and spend it with Raina. But as I climbed the hill from parking, I saw her sitting on the bleachers at the basketball court, watching the players and talking with a few folk.

She saw me too, and nodded curtly as she turned back to her friends, dismissing me. I tried to catch up with her all afternoon, but she was obviously avoiding me, and so I sat alone on the bench outside of security, watching the wimmin congregate at the mess hall for the final concert and party of the weekend.

I had relieved the staff of duty and thanked them. They hurried over to the show, leaving me alone.

The night was clear, the air cool. I could hear the wimmin clapping as the show began. The jazz band was playing. I was lonely. I felt like crying.

A figure moved slowly toward me, and as it separated from the other shadows, I saw it was

Raina. She was wearing jeans and a flannel shirt as protection against the night breeze.

"How's it going? Coming to the show?"

"I can't. Someone has to cover the phones. I let everyone else go." My eyes filled with tears. If Raina noticed, she didn't show it. She sat beside me and looked out across the land.

"Mind a little company?" She pulled out a joint, not caring that I was head of security, and lit it. Taking a long drag, she blew it out slowly, studying the orange ember thoughtfully.

"You know, you deserved to be a part of this festival as much as anyone—probably more, because you worked so long putting it together. But you spent the entire weekend taking care of everyone—everyone but you."

She took another toke and then handed it to me. What the hell? I took a couple of hits and then handed it back to her.

She filled her lungs a final time and then flicked it away. Turning to me, she placed her hands on my shoulders. "So. What say we take care of you right now?" She kissed me lightly and then pulled back. "How does that sound?"

I know it sounds silly, but her gentle voice and generous gesture unlocked the flood gate of disappointment, frustration, and anger that had been pent up all weekend, and I burst into tears.

Raina tenderly kissed my face. Her lips fluttered over my eyes, cheek, chin, all the while stroking my hair and making soothing sounds deep in her throat.

The drumming circle had begun. The primal rhythms pulsed through the darkness. My heart was beating too, as Raina stood and took my hand. "Come on."

I saw feminine images, writhing with the ecstasy summoned by the drums, moving in the windows of the mess, as Raina led me up the stairs and into the security building.

She locked the door and turned out the porch light. I started, "What if someone . . ." but she shushed me. Going into the office, she took the phone off the hook and put it in the desk drawer before closing that room off.

She turned to me then, and unhooked the walkie-talkie from my belt, calmly removing the batteries and dropping them into her pouch before tossing the radio on the table.

"Now. Is this where you sleep?"

"Yes," was all I could manage.

She took my hand again and led me into the dark room. I reached for the light switch, but she stopped me. "Candles?" she asked.

"No. Sorry."

"That's fine. This will do." She pulled out her flashlight and turned it on, standing it on the shelf near the cot. The light reflected off the ceiling, casting a dim light in the room. She lit three sticks of incense before turning back to me.

She slowly unbuttoned my shirt, and said as she bent forward, "I've wanted to do this all weekend. Well, better late than . . ." as she cupped by breasts, bringing them one and then the other to her mouth. She rubbed her face between them, wetting my hardened nipples with the tip of her tongue.

My hands reached through her thick, heavy locks, to massage her scalp and hold her to me as she nuzzled my increasingly sensitive breasts.

She explored my body, using her fingers as her eyes. "Precious, so precious," she whispered as she knelt before me and kissed my belly. Her hands moved to my pants as her eyes studied mine for acquiescence.

I held my breath and nodded as she worked the elastic waistband over my hips and pushed them to the floor. She gave me her hand for support, as I stepped out of them and kicked them aside.

"Ahhh." she breathed, as she leaned forward, inhaling the musky scent of my arousal. She stroked and pulled on my fleshy outer lips, brushing my swollen hood carelessly with a knuckle.

I shuddered at that touch—electrified. She kissed my thighs, my knees, my calves before rising up, over my belly, breasts, neck, ears.

We kissed again, intensity building. I unbuttoned her shirt and moved closer, breast to breast, as she shrugged it to the floor.

As she ravaged my mouth with her tongue, her teeth, I breathlessly unzipped her jeans. She pushed them down and stepped out of them as she backed me to the cot, gently guiding me back on the cushioned surface.

She stood, poised above me, studying my naked body in the dim light, a small smile playing at the corners of her mouth.

"Why are you laughing?" I said, suddenly embarrassed.

"I'm not laughing." She said, still smiling. "You're just very beautiful. So sweet. May I . . . taste you?" Her voice was quiet, tense.

I blushed and nodded shyly, parting my legs slightly.

She straddled me, kneading my thighs and leaning forward to kiss me again, playfully nibbling my lower lip before trailing down my body, finally settling herself between my trembling thighs. She rubbed her face in my drenched hairs and then ran her tongue along the inner rim of my dripping canal.

Someone knocked on the door and shouted my name. "Hey, you in there?" My body tensed, ready to jump up, but Raina was over me. She put a hand over my mouth, her other hand teasing my throbbing pussy.

The knocking stopped; the person went away. Raina smiled triumphantly and disappeared between my thighs again. Suddenly, her tongue, a dull point, thrust into my hole again and again as her nose put gentle, consistent pressure on my engorged clit. Her hands gripped and squeezed my ass, my inner thighs, as she pulled me down, down on to her.

Raina parted my outer lips, revealing the slick, pink flesh beneath and began lapping in long, steady strokes. I could hear her slurping, so wet was I. She rubbed her thumb on my throbbing hood, and my body started bucking as an orgasm quickly swelled and overcame me.

She came up, laying her full weight on me, and shared my juices in a long kiss. Then she leaned up with a smile. "Happy festival. We had to take care of that first. Now we can go more slowly and get to know each other."

$$\lambda \ \lambda \ \lambda$$

The first light of dawn was creeping across the floor when Raina got up and turned off the flashlight and then jumped back under the covers, huddling near me for warmth. We dozed for an hour or so before the sounds of the drums awoke us.

The drummers were making their way through the camp offering thanks to the Mother for the space. The festival goers were packed, some had already departed, while others were climbing aboard a bus amidst hugs and kisses. Still others had gathered in the Commons around the drummers, jumping and swaying in a final celebratory dance.

Raina and I strolled over, and I stood on the outer edge of the circle as Raina joined it, picking up a shakera that she raised over her head and played vigorously as she danced. Her eyes were closed, her face turned to the morning sky, peaceful and calm. Then she turned to me, smiling, hand outstretched, summoning me to her.

I hesitated for only a moment. Feeling happy and free, I moved into the circle, closer to the dancers spinning and swaying on the green, green grass. It started raining, cold drops of water cleansing the land, soaking the earth with the spirits of the wimmin who had lived on it for four glorious days. I embraced Raina and joined the dance.

SUMMER

Flying down the highway in an open Jeep, sticky cream dripping down my arm from a melting cone of Häagen Daz. Stereo blasting.

We spent the day at the beach. Skin hot, bodies young and limber, grains of sand clinging to backs of thighs.

The ocean was warm that day, remember? We splashed into the blue-green waters. The waves were high, drenching us, but we kept going out—out.

Was there anyone else there that day? We really didn't care. We were free. It was summer. Laughing, we took off our tops and tied them to our waists, hoping they wouldn't wash away as we embraced. I wrapped my legs around you, floating on the currents, and played with your tender, freckled breasts, which bobbed just above the surface of the sea.

Your hands dove into the water, bravely seeking my cavern, exploring, finding a treasure chest I'd thought I'd lost. You broke it open and found my pearl, liberating me.

λ λ λ

On the white, burning sands you lay—looking up at the sky, clear, azure blue. There was music playing somewhere—I knew the song—though I can't recall the name now. Closing my eyes I could hear the surf, the call of gulls overhead. The sun was hot—so hot.

I rubbed oil into your golden skin, kneading your flesh with my hands. Holding the bottle over you, a trail of oil sizzled down your belly, and I allowed the last drops to fall into your sandy pubic hair.

I massaged you, the sun on my back as I worked. You traced an ice cube across my over-hanging breasts, catching the melted drops of water on your tongue. Across my chest, up in the hollow of my throat and around my lips you brushed the cube before allowing its coolness in my mouth to drip down my throat.

Still I worked on your beautiful, burning body. Lower, lower my hands circled, until my fingers dipped into your moist valley. And when your earth moved, I slipped, falling into your dark abyss.

I went down, down into that damp, secret forest. I bathed in your sweet pool. Searching for its source I journeyed on, slowly, carefully licking, tasting the waters until you swelled, and I was lost in your tidal wave.

The seagulls brought me back. It was time for us to go. A breeze off the ocean whispered, "Autumn is coming! Autumn is coming!"

We gathered our things. As we walked from the beach, the grains of sand fell from us, one by one. I turned to you—one last look at summer—but you were gone.

HONEY EYES

The early morning sun peeked through the bamboo shades and, like a million precious gems, shot brilliant prisms of color across the room. The light reflected in my lover's eyes, and I was lost in the depths of her sweet, honey-colored gaze.

She leaned over me, her breath blowing against my skin like a welcomed breeze. "I love you," she whispered, as her lips met mine. We kissed. Our lips, our tongues, our spirits touched. Her arms were around me, even as my own pulled her closer to me. Fingertips brushed skin still damp from lovemaking. I kissed her shoulder, her neck, and felt myself shiver with renewing passion. Laying her back against the pillows, I gazed upon her beautiful nakedness. I wanted her.

I took her breast in my mouth, feeling her nipple harden as I flicked it with my tongue. My fingers danced across her other breast and then trailed down, down to silky hair, curly and wet. Down, down to her heat, to her well of creamy desire.

I was drawn into her fire—like a moth I moved to her flame. Knowing that I would be consumed, yet unable to resist, not wanting to resist, I flew closer and closer—dizzy with the ever growing scent of *her*.

And then I was there. I lost myself in the smell, the taste of her. I drenched my face in the wetness of her.

I wanted to make her cum.

I wanted to make her thighs tremble. I wanted to see beads of perspiration form on breasts heaving with gasps of excitement. I wanted to hear her moan, deep and low, in the back of her throat as orgasm overwhelmed her.

My tongue began its hunt, exploring her folds and crevasses for the ultimate prize. And when I found it, I thrashed, and stroked and pulled it. I sucked and rolled it on my tongue and thrilled as it began to swell.

She was watching me eat her, and I could see her eyes, always so full of love, now also filling with passion. She wanted more. I wanted to give her more.

Shifting my body, careful not to lose the precious jewel locked in my mouth, I put a finger into her throbbing hole. At the same time, my other hand flew to my own aching pussy and began to stroke. She clamped down as I inserted another finger, and then another. As she rode my hand, she ground her cunt into my mouth and I felt stinging pain, tasted salty blood as I lashed at her harder, faster. I couldn't stop, even as the tender skin of my lips broke against my teeth. I didn't care. And neither did she.

Her head was thrown back, her eyes closed. One arm reached over her head, the sheets bunched in her clenched fist. The other hand, and her (yes, trembling) thighs, which had been my guide, were thrown off. I was out of control; I would not be contained. My thumb moved up to replace my tongue. I wanted to generate more pressure, more speed. I pumped her harder, faster.

She was moaning now, English forgotten. She loved me, cursed me, encouraged me in her hot, native tongue. "*Ay . . . metamela . . . si, mi amor, si . . . aaaahhhh . . . que rico, mami . . . ayyyy . . . ayyyyy . . . coño!*" Her breasts, beaded with perspiration, rose and fell sharply.

I was above her, watching her beloved face. A little line was etched between her brows, her mouth slightly parted, her breath growing more ragged as her body anticipated orgasm.

Faster, harder, deeper I plunged. And when she exploded, her body jumped from the mattress, her thighs tightened around me, crushing, as she rode the wave of release.

I could feel a fresh flood of her precious juices soak my hand, and though I was reluctant to tear my eyes from her face, I couldn't let her liquid treasure flow out and on to mere sheets. I moved down again and drank. And then licked, softly, as her body calmed.

She looked at me then. The light was brighter now, the sounds of the awakening outside world drifting into the silent room.

I wanted to cry, I felt so happy, but that would have been silly, right? So instead, I moved up and into her arms and we lay together. Our breathing began to slow and we drifted off to sleep, wrapped in a blanket of love and warm Florida sunshine.

THE EXIT

They had been dating for almost three months before Alison agreed to come over to Renee's house. Three months of dinners, concerts, movies. Of museums and walks through the City. Three months of kisses and warm hugs good night—and nothing more.

Alison was great company. She was an intelligent, witty conversationalist, a compassionate listener. But Renee wanted more. Sure she valued Alison's ear, but there were other, more juicy parts of Alison's anatomy that Renee wanted to conversate with.

So when Alison finally agreed to come over, Renee was excited. She would take it easy—perhaps Alison was shy.

It was Sunday. Alison came by late in the morning for brunch. They sat around eating, sipping mimosas, talking. They watched a movie, had coffee, talked some more.

Alison looked content, relaxed. She was sitting back, eyes closed, shoulder lightly touching Renee's.

They were discussing their busy schedules when Renee decided to take her chance. She leaned over and kissed Alison, starting with a simple pressing of the lips. When Alison didn't resist her, she ran her tongue around the rim of Alison's sweet mouth, before gently pressing through her pliant lips.

Tips of tongues flickered. Alison trembled and pressed closer, seeking more. But Renee wanted to take it slowly. Withdrawing from Alison's mouth, she kissed its corners and up Alison's jaw. She rolled Alison's lobe between her teeth, lightly pulling, and then darted her tongue quickly in and out of Alison's receptive ear. She was rewarded for her efforts when a little "Oh!" escaped Alison's parted lips.

Renee ran her hands over Alison's soft, rounded body. She could feel the curves of Alison's ample flesh through the thin fabric of her dress. Massaging Alison's heavy breasts, Renee molded and squeezed the ripe orbs. She could feel the nipples hardening, even through the smoothing restraints of Alison's bra.

Alison was breathing audibly, and she gasped as Renee's hand moved down to her thighs, firmly squeezing them from the knee and higher, higher. At the same time, Renee guided Alison back into the pillows until Alison was supine.

Renee kissed her more insistently, and Alison matched her passion. Renee's hand slid even further up Alison's thigh—and came upon a bulge where Alison's thighs met.

Alison sat up quickly, embarrassed, and closed her legs, smoothing her dress over her knees. "I'm sorry. I—I have my period."

Renee sat up too. "It's okay. We'll just put a towel under you."

Alison stood up. "Oh, no. It'd be so messy. I couldn't do that."

Renee stood too. "Not a problem. But there are a few things I can do for you—and still leave your, um, pad intact."

Alison hesitated, "I don't know . . ."

Renee wasn't going to miss her chance. She took Alison's hand and pushed her gently back to the couch. "I want to make you feel good. Trust me. We'll stop immediately if you feel uncomfortable, okay? Now wait right there. I'll be back in a sec."

She returned moments later, carrying a long, colorful drawstring bag, which she opened, pulling out a Magic Wand. She wrapped its head with a face cloth and then tossed the bag aside.

"Have you ever tried this?" Renee asked Alison as she plugged in the toy.

"No." Alison answered, watching Renee dubiously.

"Then you're in for a real treat."

Renee sat on the couch beside Alison. "Lie back," she commanded. Alison complied.

Switching the wand to its "low" setting, Renee placed it firmly on Alison's mound. Alison jumped at the unexpected tingling. Renee manipulated the head in a slow, circular motion, pushing on the hood of Alison's clit, watching Alison's reactions carefully.

Alison's eyes were closed. She bit her lip and moaned back in her throat, as the vibrations stimulated her pussy. Renee was massaging Alison's breasts and murmuring words of encouragement as Alison let herself go with the feelings.

It wasn't long before Alison felt the pleasurable edge of an impending orgasm. Renee watched Alison's face flush, and realizing she was on the edge, Renee kept the toy firmly in one spot. At the same time, she leaned over, tonguing Alison's mouth feverishly. Renee's hand reached beneath Alison's bra, flicking lightly the hard nipples with her thumb nail. Alison came. Wave after wave, her body shook as orgasm pulsed through her.

Renee groaned with lust, watching Alison come so beautifully, so completely, before her. She moved the toy from Alison's pussy for a moment and straddled her. Then, turning the vibrator to high she pressed it against the thicker portion of Alison's pad for less direct contact and positioned herself over Alison's body. Lying fully on Alison, the vibrator stimulating both of them, Renee began slowly grinding her hips against Alison's mound.

Alison learned fast and wanted more. She wrapped her legs around Renee, opening herself further and bringing Renee closer, giving them both better contact with the wand. It wasn't long before they both came.

Renee put the wand into its bag and turned to Alison who, with one arm thrown over her eyes, was still recovering from the new sensations she had experienced.

"I'm going to take a shower. Why don't you join me? We can order something for dinner after."

"Sounds good. I'm right behind you." Alison sat up as Renee went into the bathroom.

λ λ λ

The room was filling with steam and Renee was already under the water when Alison entered. She stripped quickly and tossed her pad into the trash as she stepped into the shower. They washed each other, talking and laughing. Renee got out first, while Alison washed her hair.

When Alison stepped out of the shower, Renee confronted her. "You lied to me."

Dripping wet, shivering, Alison said, "Can I have a towel? What did I lie about?"

Renee ignored her request and instead pointed to the trash can. "You're not on your period."

Alison was embarrassed. "Oh . . . I was . . . I was protecting myself. I—I wasn't sure I was prepared to get intimate with you. I was—well, I was scared."

Renee's voice lowered. "Did I hurt you?"

"No."

Renee stepped closer. "Was I not gentle with you at any time?"

Alison looked at Renee warmly. "You were very gentle and considerate."

"Have I given you any reason to lie to me?"

Alison stuttered "No . . . no, I was being silly. Can I . . . can I have a towel?"

Renee got her a towel from the closet. Watching Alison dry off, she said, "You know you're going to have to pay for that."

Alison rubbed oil on her legs. "What? I apologized. Don't be mad."

Renee smiled slightly as she hugged Alison. "I'm not angry."

λ λ λ

Wrapped in towels, Renee went to the kitchen to pour wine, while Alison sat on the sofa and waited. They chatted for a while as they drained their glasses. Then Renee set them aside and moved closer to Alison, aggressively taking Alison into her arms and kissing her deeply. Alison responded eagerly.

Renee pushed Alison back against the pillows and tore open her towel, running her hands roughly all over Alison's body, pulling and twisting Alison's nipples, while she savaged her mouth.

Breathless, excited, Alison responded to this more assertive approach by parting her legs so that Renee could lie on her, thigh pressed against her aching pussy, Renee's juices lubricating her leg.

Renee got up. "I'll be right back." She went to her closet and took something out, then slipped into the bathroom. Alison traced circles in the wet spots on her thighs while she waited for Renee to return.

Moments later, Renee emerged from the bathroom in full harness and nine-inch dildo.

Tossing Alison a foil packet, Renee told her to "put it on me."

Alison knelt before Renee and, with trembling fingers, rolled the condom down the thick shaft. Renee pulled Alison's head closer and ordered her to kiss it.

Alison hesitated for just a moment, and then complied. She kissed and licked its length, took the bulbous head in her mouth and sucked it.

"You like that don't you?" Renee hissed as she pushed Alison back. Alison, sprawled on the carpeted floor, opening her arms and legs to welcome Renee into her. Renee lay on top of Alison, careful not to penetrate Alison's glistening, starving hole.

She pressed the dildo between Alison's sticky folds and slid it back and forth, driving Alison mad.

"Suddenly, Renee stood. "Wait, come with me."

"Where are we going?" Alison asked as she took Renee's hand.

"Shhh. Close your eyes, it's a surprise." Renee said as she led Alison through the kitchen. "Take five steps forward and turn. Count to ten and then open your eyes."

Alison giggled as she complied with Renee's instructions. She started counting, and at eight she heard a door slam. Opening her eyes, she was stunned to find that she was standing in the public hallway near the service elevator—completely naked!

She tapped on the door and whispered, "Renee—let me in! This isn't funny."

She heard Renee snickering on the other side of the door.

"Why are you doing this? Renee? Renee?"

Alison heard the elevator doors open around the corner. Seeing the brightly lit EXIT sign, she ducked into the stairwell just in time to see a womon, arms heavy with groceries, pass by. She could hear keys, a door opening, silence.

Bewildered, heart pounding, Alison was about to peek into the hallway when she heard the sound of footsteps approaching the stairs. There was nowhere to hide. The footsteps stopped right outside the door!

"Alison?" The door opened. It was Renee, wearing a robe.

Alison burst into tears. "That wasn't funny! I can't believe you did that."

Renee folded Alison in her arms, stroking her hair, kissing the salty drops on her cheeks. "I'm sorry. Oh, baby it's okay, baby. Shhh..."

Renee kissed Alison gently, tiny kisses all over her tear-stained face. When she got to Alison's lips, Alison kissed her back urgently. Renee's body throbbed in response. She returned Alison's kisses, which grew more passionate as Alison's sobs diminished.

"Oh baby... shhh... okay... okay... yes baby." Renee whispered over and over.

Their hands were everywhere, touching, pulling at each other. They slammed up against the exit door, Alison pressing her aching pussy against the hard bulge of the dildo Renee was still wearing. Renee grabbed Alison's ass, and Alison moaned as Renee's robe parted, the thick rod slipping between Alison's thighs.

The elevator opened. Renee clamped a hand over Alison's mouth, but continued to suck on her neck, to slide the dildo back and forth along the outer rim of Alison's slick canal.

They could hear, and then see, a rowdy group of kids with skateboards pass them. A womon pushing a stroller followed them, shouting at them to keep their voices down.

Alison lifted a leg and wrapped it around Renee's waist and Renee sank her rod into Alison, pumping her slowly and deeply, the pleasure more intense, because they were struggling to remain silent.

Alison couldn't help herself. A moan escaped. And grabbing Renee's harness, she manipulated the leather straps to add pressure on Renee's clit, as

Renee fucked her harder and deeper, faster and faster.

Renee struggled out of her robe and let it drop to the floor. Then, careful not to lose contact, she and Alison sank to the floor.

Alison lifted her hips, and Renee slipped her hands beneath Alison's ass, dictating the speed and depth of each thrust. They were lost, moaning and panting.

Alison's body bucked. "Yes . . . yessss . . ." she chanted, as she started cumming.

Grabbing Renee's ass hard, Alison fingered Renee's tight nether hole frantically, as her body continued jerking in ecstasy.

Watching Alison's face contort in spasms of orgasm, and having her asshole teased sent Renee over the edge. Within moments, Renee came too.

They lay there breathless, sweaty, when they heard someone coming up the stairs. Remembering where they were, Renee peeked into the hallway and then gave Alison the 'all's clear' signal. They made a mad dash for the apartment. Slamming the door behind them, they collapsed in each other's arms in a fit of laughter.

PONGEE

It had been a long, aggravating day. Kimberly slumped in the back seat of the cab as it headed across town to her hotel. Thank god she was going home in the morning. Massaging her temples, Kimberly tried to alleviate the tension headache that was painfully gripping her. Maybe a drink. . . . She suddenly remembered a little bar in the Village she'd used to go to on Friday nights once upon a time looking for . . . . She chuckled. Well, that was a long time ago. But maybe a drink for old times sake.

More than ten years had passed since Kimberly had left New York. She wasn't even sure the bar would still be there, but she gave the driver the address anyway, and crossed her fingers.

It was. Although it was mid-January, holiday lights still twinkled merrily in the window, as if welcoming her back. A flood of memories rushed to her as she entered the tavern and took in its dim interior, virtually unchanged in a decade. It was still early, the bar fairly deserted. It would be at least an hour before the after work crowd started spilling in.

Shaking out of her coat, she hung it on a hook, took a seat at the bar and ordered a vodka and tonic.

The drink was placed before her, and Kimberly took a sip, sighing as the icy liquid burned her throat and warmed her body. She savored the sensation as she willed her tension to melt from her.

λ λ λ

A womon, older than Kimberly by sixteen years, sat at a corner table nursing a beer. She wore faded black jeans over cowboy boots, a denim shirt tucked in under a studded leather jacket. Beadwork in the style of her ancestors, the Apsaroke, decorated her ears, neck and wrists. Her hair, crew cut on top, long and straight down her back, was starkly white.

She studied the womon at the bar, wondering if she would remember. It had been a long time. Finally, she rose and crossed the floor.

Kimberly watched the womon make her way over in the reflection of the mirror. Her heart was pounding at the sight of the white hair. As the figure stepped from the shadows and into the light, Kimberly gripped the bar.

The womon placed a hand on Kimberly's shoulder. "You do remember."

Kimberly looked at the reflection in the mirror. "Pongee."

Pongee took the stool beside Kimberly and ordered another beer. "Something for you?" Her eyes were steady, unwavering as she studied Kimberly.

Tears welled in Kimberly's eyes as she nodded and looked away, whispering, "Yes, another of the same."

λ λ λ

Pongee was a professor at the law school Kimberly had attended. Kimberly remembered seeing Pongee in the halls or sometimes, late at night, in the library. She found something about the striking Native American intriguing. She was infatuated by her strong, dominating presence.

One Friday night Kimberly had decided to follow Pongee and found herself in this little wimmin's bar. Kimberly found a seat at the corner of the bar and ordered. For hours she had sat in the shadows watching the tall, strong womon move through the crowds, accepting hearty welcomes and warm hugs from the other wimmin, until she was aching with desire to touch Pongee herself.

Kimberly was obsessed. For several weeks, she stopped in at the bar on Friday nights after class, ordered a beer, and waited—knowing that Pongee would be in at some point. She would watch Pongee drink, talk, dance with the wimmin, and she would fantasize about Pongee's lips pressed against hers, Pongee's body covering her own, and her body would throb.

Kimberly knew that someone like Pongee could never even notice her, so Kimberly had never approached her. The few times Pongee's gaze fell on her, Kimberly would blush and look away.

Then one night, just as Kimberly was leaving the bar, Pongee caught her at the door. Pongee placed her hand lightly on the small of Kimberly's back as she asked her to join for her for a coffee at a nearby diner.

Seated across from each other, mugs of steaming black brew before them, Pongee got to the point. "You've been following me." Her dark eyes inscrutable.

Kimberly looked into her coffee. "Yes," she whispered.

Pongee leaned forward, touching Kimberly's arm. "Why?"

Feeling cornered and ridiculous, Kimberly burst into tears. She gushed, "because—because I thought you could. . . . I mean I think you're just . . ." she faded into embarrassed silence.

Pongee smiled slightly as she lit a cigarette and took a long, thoughtful drag. She studied this child-womon before her. Kimberly was fresh, beautiful and vulnerable—very erotic. Pongee knew she would enjoy having her, but for some reason, Kimberly touched Pongee's somewhat jaded heart. She asked gently, "Have you ever been with a womon before?"

Kimberly stuttered, "Well . . . no . . . not . . . um . . . exactly."

Pongee smiled. "And you want me to be the first."

Kimberly looked directly into Pongee's eyes. "I just thought . . . that is—well, you seem so *experienced*. I don't know. So sure of yourself. I know you'd know what to do."

Pongee chuckled. "Yeah, well, I suppose I do. But your first time with a womon should be special—with someone you trust and care about. Look. I don't generally do this, but I am going to give you some advice. Take it easy. Why don't we try being friends, get to know each other. If and when the time is right for us to be together in that way—I promise it will be very special."

λ λ λ

But that time had never come. Kimberly's father had a stroke less than two months later, and Kimberly flew home to Los Angeles. She stayed on to care for him and finished her last year of law school there. After passing the California bar exam, she had joined her father's firm.

She met Lynn at a law convention, and they started dating. When Kimberly's father died a few years later, Kimberly invited Lynn into the firm and her home. Her life was good. They were happy. But Kimberly had never forgotten Pongee.

Sometimes when she and Lynn were making love, Kimberly would close her eyes and see Pongee's penetrating, obsidian eyes gazing at her. She imagined Pongee's strong, square hands moving knowingly over her body, taking her to the edge—and over. Was it fate that had now brought them together again?

The bartender set the drinks down and moved away. Pongee spoke. "Have you moved back to the City?" Her voice was low and steady.

Kimberly's body throbbed in response. "No . . . no, I'm just in this week for meetings. In fact, I fly out tomorrow morning early."

Pongee sipped her drink in silence.

"How have you been? I mean . . . are you happy?" Kimberly asked, her voice trembling.

Pongee finished her draft and pushed the glass aside before placing her hand over Kimberly's. "Yes, I am happy. Happy to have found you again, if only for one night. Do we have tonight, Kimberly?"

Kimberly thought of Lynn, her lover, her partner. She thought of the life they had created together over the years. They were very happy.... She turned to Pongee and took a deep breath. "There is nothing in the world I want more."

Pongee tossed some money on the bar and, getting Kimberly's coat, guided her out into the night.

λ λ λ

The maid had already been in to turn down the bed. A lamp in the bedroom was left on, its light spilling into the living area where Kimberly and Pongee removed their coats. Kimberly kicked off her pumps and padded over to the wet bar. "Drink?"

"No."

Kimberly took out a beer, nervously fumbling with the top. Finally popping the cap and dropping it in the trash, she placed the frosty bottle against her flaming forehead with a shaky hand, willing herself to calm down. She was no longer an infatuated child, insecure and inexperienced, Kimberly admonished herself. She had no reason to be nervous. Resolutely, she turned.

Pongee was sitting on the couch, calmly studying Kimberly. Her arms were outstretched along the back of the sofa.

"Are you sure this is okay for you?" Pongee asked as Kimberly sat beside her. Her voice was liquid, hypnotic.

Kimberly sighed, leaning back into Pongee's protective arms. "I can't tell you how many times over the years I've thought about you—how it might have been. So many things have changed in my life, Pongee. I've changed. But you . . . you're just like you were the last time I saw you."

Pongee took the bottle from Kimberly and put it on the table. She shook her head somberly and answered in a quiet voice. "I've changed too, Kimberly."

She continued more strongly, "But for tonight, for these few precious hours, let's forget everything and everyone. This is our time. Yours and mine." She leaned forward, gently kissing Kimberly's forehead. "We're long overdue."

Kimberly closed her eyes as Pongee kissed her lids, her cheeks, the corners of her mouth, before drawing back. Pongee cupped Kimberly's chin and gazed into her eyes. She saw hunger reflected there, and need and desire.

Pongee kissed Kimberly. Visions of snowy mountains and pine forests flashed in Kimberly's mind as she took in Pongee's scent. Her lips parted as Pongee's tongue sought entry. Kimberly surrendered to her. There was no other world than this.

Pongee pressed closer, her strong arms pulling Kimberly to her, her tongue becoming more demanding, insistent. Kimberly responded with a deep moan of desire.

Pongee nibbled Kimberly's ear, her neck—tiny bites, sharp, making Kimberly's center throb with desire. Kimberly gasped as Pongee's hand found its way through the barriers of blouse and bra, to fondle Kimberly's heavy, sensitive breasts.

Withdrawing from Pongee's embrace, her heart racing, Kimberly stood. She removed her blouse, tossed it aside, and then unbuttoned and stepped out of her skirt. She stripped slowly, layer by layer, her eyes never leaving Pongee's, until she stood before her, naked.

Pongee drank in the sight of Kimberly's ripe, rounded flesh. Reverently, her hands not quite touching Kimberly, Pongee traced an outline of Kimberly's body. She was breathing deeply, steadily, as she made her way over Kimberly's head and face, shoulders and breasts. She knelt, inhaling the exotic aroma of Kimberly's heightening excitement, and traced her hips and thighs, calves and ankles, finally kissing the tops of Kimberly's manicured feet.

Rising, Pongee took Kimberly's hand and led her to the bedroom.

λ λ λ

Dimming the light to a romantic glow, Kimberly moved to Pongee and started unbuttoning Pongee's denim shirt. Pongee caught Kimberly's hand and stepped away. She sat on the bed to remove her pants and boots. Then, standing and turning away, Pongee removed her shirt. Wearing only her beads and a small medicine bag secured around her neck by a strip of rawhide, Pongee again faced Kimberly.

Kimberly looked sharply up into Pongee's eyes for a moment, and then back to the long scar where once Pongee's left breast had been. Kimberly knelt before Pongee and ran her finger over the slightly raised line before leaning forward to place tender kisses along its length, loving it and Pongee the more for having survived to share it with her. Then she turned her mouth to Pongee's conical right breast and suckled her hardened nub.

Pongee helped Kimberly to her feet. They held each other close for a moment and then, together, sank slowly to the bed.

λ λ λ

When Kimberly awoke, Pongee was gone. A brilliant white dove's feather lay on the pillow beside her.

λ λ λ

Kimberly directed the cabbie to take the George Washington Bridge across to New Jersey. At its center she asked him to stop and wait while she got out. Kimberly stood shivering at the railing watching the grays and lavenders of a New York winter dawn. She knew she would not be to the City again, at least not for many years.

With tears of loss, of love, of completion, Kimberly pressed the feather to her breast and then released it. She watched it drift slowly down to the water and float away.

WINTER

Your bags were packed and at the door, but the airport was shut down. We had one more night—blessed be.

The world was silent, wrapped in a soft blanket of ceaselessly falling snow. It lay pure, clean on the black branches of the trees outside my window.

We lit candles. Their circles of light reflected in the panes of glass, casting a golden halo around the two wimmin entwined in each other's arms. I was happy. I was sad. You live so far away from me. In another world.

When you are here, we step out of place and time. We move into a universe that is ours—alone. The sun, the moon, and everything beneath them are created by us, to feed our spirits.

I turn to you. Your eyes round, liquid, framed with long, thick lashes are solemn but filled with love. You know too—how little time we have. Your hand, square and wide—an artist's hand—reaches up to catch a tear, before it falls from my eye.

"Come." You lead me into the living room. We kneel so close that I can feel your breath on my cheek. "*Yo te quiero*," you whisper into my ear, touching my cheek with your warm, sweet lips.

I hold you tightly—wondering if I could ever capture this moment on paper. I wish for a pen—a fleeting thought as you bring me back to the now with your caress. You cup my breast and bow your head to it.

Sometimes, late at night, I can still feel the sensation of your tongue, your teeth, pulling, marking my skin.

"No! No!" I cry. I've already said goodbye to you in my heart. I can't—I can't let myself have this moment. It hurt so much the first time.

We stand and together go to the kitchen and look out at the snow. There are lights in the windows across the way. Lives being lived. There are no promises of tomorrow. We are given only today. Only now.

I turn to you. Yes. This is *our* time. Our moment.

Hand in hand, we go to the bedroom.

I don't need to write this down. My heart will remember.

HONEYMOON COTTAGE

"Hey, wake up." Sonia nudged the dozing womon whose head rested in her lap.

"Ummm . . . did I fall asleep?" Hillary sat up, stretching one arm over her head as she stifled a yawn with the other.

Sonia stood, reaching for her coat. "Yeah, you fell asleep—again."

Hillary studied Sonia's expression. "You're mad at me, aren't you?"

Picking up her satchel, Sonia headed for the door. "If you were too tired for company, you should have said so. I could have made other plans for tonight."

"Oh, come on. I didn't *mean* to fall asleep. It's just been a long day at the end of a long week."

"Yeah? Well it's always a 'long day' these days, and frankly, I'm tired of hearing about it."

Hillary walked over to Sonia and put her arms around her neck. "I just . . ."

"Mom?" A young voice called from the other room.

Hillary turned away, "Yes, honey?"

Sonia twisted from Hillary's grip and reached for the doorknob.

"Sonia—come on. Can't we talk about this?"

"Mom—*COME HERE!*" the pitch rose to a plaintive whine.

"Better go make sure he's okay."

Hillary looked pleadingly at Sonia, then at the door leading to her son's bedroom. "Okay. But don't leave. I'll be right back. I'm coming, honey." Hillary hurried to the back.

Sonia dropped her bag and leaned against the door.

Hillary came out. "One minute—he just wants a glass of water." She went to the kitchen and then, with glass, returned to the rear of the apartment. A few seconds later she reemerged, wiping her hands on her jeans.

"Okay, where were we?"

Sonia picked up her bag and flung it over her shoulder. "I was leaving so you could get some rest." She said the last sarcastically.

"You're not being fair, Sonia. I work every day, have a ten-year-old son to look after, and I'm busting my ass trying to get through this last semester of my master's program. You have no idea how much energy all that takes."

"No, I don't. But what I *do* know is that I have a demanding career, requiring a regular seventy-hour week. I chair an active, hands-on board of directors and volunteer time at the community hotline. But despite all of that, not to mention a five-day workout regimen, I still find time to spend with you—because *you* are a priority in my life.

"Now when I met you, you were working, had a son, and went to school. But you also said you wanted a relationship and made time to be with me. Now, I get dinner in the kitchen discussing Terrence's homework, family television in the living room until Terrence's bedtime, and then five minutes of grown-up talk before you zonk out. Add to that the fact that we've made love *twice* in the past six weeks, and I'd say I had damned good reason to be pissed."

Hillary flopped in a chair, wearily brushing her eyes. She looked up at Sonia and said in a tired voice, "I know I've been distracted. I just feel so overwhelmed. I'm doing the best I can—you just don't understand how hard it is to juggle all of these responsibilities."

Sonia refused to give in. "Look. I want you to take care of your life. But I have a responsibility to see that my needs are being met, and they're not—not the way things stand. There was a time when we spent time together *alone*. Just us. Making love, hanging out—but no more. Why is that?"

Hillary shook her head. "I don't know, Sonia. I don't know."

Sonia's voice softened. "I think we need to schedule time for us. Just like you schedule study groups, activist meetings, time with Terrence, brunch with friends—we need to schedule time for us. Just us. No kids, no phones, no term papers.

"It doesn't have to be every weekend—or even all weekend. But it has to be planned—no excuses, no emergencies. Is that too much to ask?"

Hillary went to Sonia. "No. It's not too much to ask at all."

Sonia sighed, smiling for the first time. "Good. Then let's set a date." She reached into her bag and pulled out her day planner.

"How 'bout next weekend—Saturday or Sunday?"

Hillary's brow furrowed. "Next weekend's bad. There's a workshop on racism I wanted to attend up in Albany next weekend."

Sonia's mouth tightened. "Fine. You tell me when you're free."

Hillary got her calendar. "Well, the weekend after that I sorta planned to take Terrence to the museum, and I have a paper to start. The weekend after that . . . maybe . . . I mean, I should have the paper done before then."

Sonia dropped her book into her bag and opened the door. "Right. Well, you do what you need to do, okay? But I'm not waiting forever. If something doesn't change soon, we're through." She turned and stalked down the hallway.

"Sonia! Sonia, come on!" Hillary called out to her, but Sonia kept going. She didn't look back.

λ λ λ

Sonia sat in her soft, caramel-colored leather chair, looking out at the lights reflecting in the waters of the Hudson. The office was dark, her computer screen giving the room a blue glow. She slipped a CD into her stereo and sat back. Sipping a cup of cappuccino, the soothing sounds of the rain forest playing softly in the background, Sonia contemplated her and Hillary's situation.

She loved that Hillary was so special a womon. Warm and concerned, she was active in the community, artistic, a good mother, *and* she could cook like nobody's business. But Sonia had been involved with ultra-busy wimmin before—their energy was like a beacon for her. It always started out fine, but eventually she felt nudged into a tiny corner of their overstuffed worlds, crowded out by seemingly more important people, events—whatever.

Well, for a change, Sonia wanted to be first. For a change, *she* wanted to be the priority. Sonia refused—REFUSED—to accept the scraps of other people's time and attention. She would no longer be just another item on anyone's "Things to Do" list.

Her intercom buzzed. "Someone here to see you, Ms. Charles."

Sonia sat up and looked at her watch, and then at her calendar which lay open on her desk. It was 5:45 p.m. She didn't have any late appointments scheduled. Leaning forward, she pushed a button, speaking into the phone mic. "Who is it, Vanessa?"

The door opened. "Do you have a minute?" Hillary stepped in, closing the door behind her. She leaned against it, holding a white paper shopping bag in front of her like a shield.

"I thought you might be hungry, so I picked up some sushi." Hillary walked uncertainly toward the desk. "I've missed you. You haven't returned any of my calls all week. Are we through without even trying to work this out? Are you ready to just forget me?" There were tears in Hillary's eyes.

Sonia pushed away from her desk and stood, pacing the floor in front of the window. "Forget you? Hillary, I haven't been able to concentrate all week. All I think about is you."

"Then why have you been avoiding me?"
Sonia sat again, burying her face in her hands. "Hillary, I love you. Sincerely. But I need more. More time, more attention. Lately, when we're together, I feel like you're thinking about all of the other, more important things you could be doing if only you didn't have to spend this hour or this night, with me. I deserve more than that."

Hillary dropped the bag on the desk as she came around and sat on Sonia's lap, hugging Sonia to her ample breast. "Oh honey, you're right. I have been taking you for granted. It's just that I have been so distracted that I've not given a thought to how this all might be affecting you. But I'm sure we can work through this, Sonia. Please say we can try."

She kissed Sonia's forehead and stroked her hair. "Please," she whispered, holding Sonia's face between her hands and gazing into her eyes. Hillary kissed Sonia softly on the lips and then pulled back, studying Sonia before kissing her again. Hillary's lips transmitted to Sonia her love and need.

Sonia's hands were at her sides, resting on the arms of the chair. Now she brought them up, circling Hillary's waist and pulling her close.

Sonia's arms gripped Hillary closer as she responded to Hillary's fervent kisses. Their mouths found each other and melted together.

Sonia's hands moved over Hillary's back, sliding over Hillary's silk blouse, squeezing Hillary's firm softness beneath.

"Oh, sweetheart." Sonia breathed as her hands moved down, stroking Hillary's stockinged calf, thigh.

Hillary hungrily kissed Sonia's jaw, neck—breathed into Sonia's ear as she kissed the place beneath it, as she pressed Sonia's face deeper into her cleavage.

Sonia took in Hillary's scent—soap, sweat, and Somalia Rose. She rubbed her face back and forth, kissing the swells peeking through the opening of Hillary's blouse.

Hillary unfastened the top buttons of Sonia's shirt and pulled it from the waistband of her tailored trousers, her hands slipping under and onto Sonia's bare skin.

Sonia parted her legs so that Hillary's bottom slipped down, leaving her suspended between Sonia's thighs and the cushion of the leather chair, pressing against Sonia's crotch.

Sonia felt her pussy pulse. It had been so long. She fed hungrily on Hillary's mouth, her tongue parting Hillary's soft lips.

Their tongues danced—joining and separating, licking and sucking. Sonia gripped Hillary's ass, pulling it closer to her crotch, even as Hillary rubbed her breasts, nipples erect, against Sonia's face.

Hillary held Sonia's neck as they kissed, her fingers playing in Sonia's thick, coarse hair. Her other hand pinched and squeezed Sonia's muscled back; her nails scraped down Sonia's spine.

Hillary parted her thighs, slipping further into the chair and against Sonia's hungering mound. Sonia reached up and under Hillary's skirt. She buried her face in Hillary's neck, murmuring "I love you. I love you." as she fingered Hillary's damp panties, feeling the heat beneath the satiny fabric.

"Oh yes, baby," Hillary urged. "Yes—touch me. I've missed you so much."

There was a knock at the door. "Ms. Charles?"

Hillary jumped up from Sonia's lap, adjusting her skirt and hair, turning to the window, her back to the door.

Sonia stuffed her shirt into her pants and took a deep breath, calling out, "Yes, Vanessa, what is it?"

Vanessa discreetly called through the closed door, "If you're done with me, I'd like to get on home. Okay?"

Hillary turned and looked at Sonia, smiling as Sonia said, "That's fine. I won't be needing you anymore tonight. Thanks—see you tomorrow."

She turned to Hillary. "Remind me to get her flowers." They laughed.

"I'm starved," Hillary said, opening the bag of raw fish. "How about some Yellowtail?"

λ λ λ

Hillary suggested a long weekend together. She conceded that racism would probably still be an issue next month. And when Hillary told Sonia that Terrence was thrilled to be spending the weekend with his cousins, Sonia borrowed a friend's place in the Berkshires. They headed out after work on Friday, stopping to pick up groceries before getting on the highway.

It was late, the road dark, dotted with the lights of cars and trucks heading for unknown destinations. Sonia turned on the radio and lit a cigarette as she hummed along.

Hillary closed her eyes, imagining what the weekend would be like—the two of them, all alone in the mountains. She pictured Sonia standing behind her in the kitchen, pressing up against her as she cooked, kissing her neck, playing with her breasts.

Her body tingled at the thought of Sonia's mouth leaving a hot, wet trail as she moved over Hillary's bare flesh, a cool breeze from an open window chilling their burning bodies.

Hillary shifted closer to Sonia and whispered "I can't wait to get there—I'm so excited."

Sonia grinned as she continued peering out at the dark road. "Yeah, me too, baby."

Hillary moved closer, putting one leg up on the dashboard. Taking Sonia's free hand, she put it between her legs. "No—I'm excited—NOW."

The car swerved as Sonia made contact with Hillary's wet—and panty-less crotch. "Shit!" Sonia swore, getting the car back under control. She glanced over at Hillary who was smiling wickedly as she hiked her skirt up and put her other leg on the dash.

"You're gonna make me crash doing that!" Sonia darted her eyes from Hillary to the road and back.

"Doing what?" Hillary asked innocently as she unbuttoned her shirt.

"You mean, taking my shirt off—like this?" She tossed the shirt in the back seat. Sonia stared at Hillary's plump breasts bursting out of her lacy bra.

"Or do you mean doing this?" She lifted her orbs from their sling, pulling on the nipples until they stood erect.

"Now don't they look suckable?" Hillary extended her tongue, flicking her own hard nubs. "Well, don't you worry about me. You just keep on driving. I can entertain myself." She dipped her fingers between her legs and played with herself.

Sonia's mouth watered. She could hear how wet Hillary was.

The car had slowed to a crawl. Sonia couldn't keep her eyes on the road as Hillary sat beside her, masturbating shamelessly.

"Ooh baby, you should feel how wet I am thinking about all the things we're gonna do this weekend." Hillary slipped a finger inside of her and pulled it out, playfully touching its slickness to Sonia's lips.

Sonia moaned. Her free hand moved over to Hillary, reaching into her dark thicket. "Oh god." Sonia gasped, closing her eyes as her hand explored Hillary's drenched valley.

"Watch the road!" Hillary shouted as the car drifted.

"Fuck this." Sonia growled, pulling over to the service lane. Putting the car in park, Sonia locked the doors and jumped on Hillary.

$\lambda\ \lambda\ \lambda$

They pulled up to the house around 3:00 a.m. Hillary had refused to redress, and she now leaned against Sonia's shoulder, snoring lightly, coat thrown over her partially clad body.

Sonia turned off the ignition and shut the headlights. Cracking a window, she looked up at the dark house as she lit a cigarette.

It was a traditional log-style cabin with a sleeping loft overlooking the living room. She had been here before, on ski weekends with her friends, so she knew that is was beautifully decorated (Hillary would like that) and extremely comfortable (that's what *she* was talking about). In addition to the master loft, there was a huge living room with fireplace, spacious eat-in kitchen, two smaller bedrooms and a full bath on the first floor. The bath in the master suite was fitted with an Italian marble Jacuzzi—the only contrast to an otherwise rustic, country motif.

During season, the area was packed with lovers of snow adventure, but now, in early March, skiing was over and it was still too cold and damp for spring jaunts, so the area was deserted.

Flicking away her stub, Sonia stroked Hillary's cheek. "We're here, Hill. Wake up. Let's go inside."

Hillary hugged Sonia's arm, opening her eyes sleepily. "Okay. I'm awake."

"Button your coat—it's chilly out. I'll get the door so you can just run in." Sonia stepped out of the car.

Hillary unrolled her window as Sonia walked by. "Unlock the trunk so we can get the groceries."

Sonia called over her shoulder as she climbed the steps, "Forget them. They'll keep 'til morning."

λ λ λ

Sonia loved sleeping in—especially when there was someone to snuggle up with. She reached out to pull Hillary to her and felt the cold, empty sheets. She rolled over and picked up her watch—11:15 a.m.

She sat up. She could hear Hillary singing below, opening cabinets, running water. Sonia smelled bacon and smiled. Good womon.

Brushing her teeth and splashing her face, Sonia threw on her discarded shirt and socks and headed downstairs. The tea kettle was whistling. Peeking into the kitchen, Sonia watched Hillary dance around as she stirred a bowl of pancake batter. Butter and syrup were on the table, along with two tall glasses of orange juice.

Hillary poured the mixture into the skillet and said, "Well, it's about time. I thought I'd have to come up and get you."

Sonia came in and sat at the table. "How'd you know I was standing there?"

Hillary wiped her hands on the towel tucked in her jeans as she came over and kissed Sonia. "I'm a mother—remember? I have eyes in the back of my head."

Sonia pulled her down to her lap. "Well, good morning—Mom." She kissed Hillary again.

"Good morning. Now let me up so I can turn these pancakes. Don't go interrupting my rhythm."

"Okay—oh—are all the groceries in?"

"Yes. I've been up for HOURS. I've unpacked, dusted the place, planned lunch, *and* balanced the nation's budget all while you snored away upstairs."

Sonia released Hillary and watched her move to the stove. "Well, how about I reward you with a nice massage later?"

"Sounds good—I deserve it." Hillary flipped the flapjacks and then went to the cabinets and reached for the plates. Sonia came up behind her, hugging her up against the counter.

"You are a good womon." she nuzzled into Hillary's neck. "Mmmm. And you smell delicious." She bit Hillary's shoulder.

"Ahhh! Cut it out you animal—I'm trying to cook."

Sonia pressed harder. "So am I." She kissed Hillary's neck and pushed her t-shirt up, caressing her breasts.

"Your pancakes are going to burn." Hillary warned, leaning back into Sonia's warm, solid body.

"I'm already burning. What are you going to do about that?"

Hillary turned to Sonia, throwing her arms around Sonia's neck. "Well, I don't know. Maybe I should flip you?" She kissed Sonia provocatively. "How hungry are you?"

Sonia's hands traveled up Hillary's sides, her thumbs brushing Hillary's breasts as she lifted Hillary to the counter. "Oh very hungry. I'm—very, very hungry."

Sonia helped Hillary ease out of her jeans and panties, and buried her face in Hillary's bush of crinkled brown hair.

Hillary closed her eyes. "But . . . but the . . . breakfast," she gasped.

Sonia reached over and turned off the gas and pushed the smoking skillet from the eye. "Ummmm. Yes. Now this is what I want for breakfast," she breathed as her mouth worked its way slowly up Hillary's inner thighs.

Hillary leaned back, resting her head against the cabinets, a sigh escaping her lips as Sonia's tongue found and dipped into Hillary's pot of sweet syrup.

λ λ λ

Sonia sat on the couch in front of the fireplace, Hillary on the floor between her legs, a bowl of grapes on Hillary's lap. Sonia held a bunch in one hand, the other hand stroking Hillary's hair, neck, and shoulders.

Hillary's eyes were closed. She felt peaceful and relaxed, savoring the cool bursts of juice and pulp on her tongue as she ate the grapes Sonia fed her.

"I feel so wonderful, Son." She took Sonia's hand, kissing the palm and then hugging it to her face.

Sonia caressed Hillary's cheek. "Me too, baby."

"It's amazing how easy it is to forget to take time out like this. Thank you."

Sonia kissed the top of Hillary's head in reply.

The fire crackled and popped, the flames creating images as the wimmin stared into them, contentedly silent.

"Hil—how 'bout I give you that massage?" Sonia squeezed Hillary's shoulder.

"Ummm—maybe a little later. I can't bear to move right now."

Sonia got up. "You stay where you are. Just get undressed and I'll take care of everything."

Sonia put two more logs on the fire and then ran upstairs to get her things. Hillary stripped and reached for the throw that was draped across the back of the sofa. Wrapping herself in the soft wool, she moved closer to the fire, enjoying the heat.

Sonia came in carrying a bag in one hand, two glasses and a bottle of wine in the other. Setting the items on the table, she uncorked the bottle and filled the glasses, handing one to Hillary.

"Start on this while I prepare." Sonia laid a towel on the floor and then unpacked her oils. She dropped another log and several pine cones into the fire, and then undressed. Kneeling beside Hillary, she picked up her glass. They clinked crystal and sipped their drinks. "Ready?" Sonia asked.

Hillary nodded.

"Then, if you please, welcome to my parlor." Sonia indicated the towel, bowing deeply. "Please be so kind as to lie here."

Hillary dropped the blanket from her and stood. "Ooh—it's a little chilly in here." Goose bumps rising on her arms.

Sonia poured oil into her hands and rubbed them together, warming the liquid. "Not for long my dear."

Hillary stretched out on the towel and closed her eyes as Sonia began stroking her arms in firm, long motions, working from the shoulder to the wrists, until Hillary's skin was smooth again.

Then Sonia's hands moved down her body, rubbing, kneading Hillary's breasts, ribs, belly, tracing the lighter lines that decorated her skin there—warrior marks of the Mother.

Sonia concentrated on her task, pushing aside the messages her own body was sending to her brain as her hands roamed Hillary's abundant flesh.

Hillary closed her eyes, giving herself over to Sonia's expert ministrations. Sonia worked steadily, feeling the points of tension in Hillary's body and releasing them. She was careful not to touch Hillary's fragrant womonhood, lest she forget herself.

Hillary moaned deep in her throat, "God, that's good." She parted her thighs, her aroused scent wafting up to Sonia, making her body throb.

Resisting temptation, Sonia took a deep breath and continued downward to Hillary's calves, ankles, feet. "Turn over now." Sonia said in a husky voice, moving aside as Hillary repositioned herself. Sonia swallowed deeply as she took in the sight of Hillary's wide, rounded ass rising up at her like a gift. She straddled Hillary's thighs and leaned forward, her own soaking, aching pussy brushing against Hillary's pliant mound as she massaged Hillary's shoulders and back. Her breathing was becoming more labored as she struggled to maintain control. Her hands moved down to Hillary's ass—she smoothed and stroked it—her mouth watering with desire.

With difficulty, Sonia moved to the backs of Hillary's thighs, but Hillary's musky scent and her oiled flesh glowing in the light of the fire overwhelmed Sonia's good intentions. Her hands, with minds of their own, traveled back up Hillary's spine and when they reached her shoulders, Sonia pressed her full body against Hillary's.

Hillary moaned "Yes," as Sonia slowly moved her pussy firmly over Hillary's ass. Sonia rested her cheek on Hillary's head, reaching beneath to finger Hillary's cunt. Hooking her finger inside Hillary's slippery hole, her thumb pressing Hillary's clit, Sonia started grinding Hillary's ass.

Hillary moved in concert with Sonia's gyrations, raising and rotating her ass. Moans of arousal escaped her lips. Her hands gripped the towel, the carpet, as she jerked her ass up against Sonia's humping pussy and back down on Sonia's fingers which slipped further inside of her.

They moved in unison, the heat from the fire and their passion making their bodies sweaty and sticky.

Sonia cried out as she exploded in orgasm. She humped Hillary's ass until the tremors died away and then moved to Hillary's side. Without withdrawing her hand from Hillary's pussy, Sonia used her other hand to manipulate Hillary's ass. She pressed her hand between Hillary's cheeks, running her fingers along the crack, around the rim of Hillary's tight, hungry hole.

Hillary, writhing on the floor, lost in the feeling of Sonia finger-fucking her pussy and ass simultaneously—came.

Sonia soothed the last spasms from Hillary's body and then lay beside her, pulling the blanket over them. Cuddling spoon-fashion, they dozed off.

λ λ λ

The room was dark. The fire had burned down to glowing embers. It was cold—that's what woke Sonia. She snuggled closer to Hillary as her eyes adjusted to the early evening gloom. She lay still, listening to Hillary's steady breathing and thanking the Universe for having brought this womon into her life. Hillary stirred.

"Are you awake?" Sonia whispered.

"Yes. I'm cold." Hillary murmured. "And hungry."

Sonia laughed, hugging Hillary closer. "It's no wonder—we burned breakfast and—uh—worked—through lunch. Why don't you get dressed while I start dinner?"

"Oooh—you're making dinner?"

"Yup. Something substantial. And no matter what—we eat dinner *as soon as it is cooked*. Deal?"

λ λ λ

Sonia was an excellent cook. Smothered chicken, collards, macaroni and cheese, sweet potatoes, cornbread, salad. Hillary came down, freshly showered, skin glowing. "Oh my! Cholesterol heaven! Yum! Yum!"

Sonia smiled. "That's right—we're being decadent this weekend. You can juice fast and get colonics for the rest of the month if you need to—but tonight, we *eat*."

λ λ λ

The table was cleared, dishes washed, food put away. They sat at the dining room table drinking coffee and sambuca, playing dominoes.

Hillary yawned as she watched her lover strategize. Sonia's brows were knitted together, she gnawed at her plump bottom lip. Hillary wanted some of that lip.

"Yes! Twenty-five." Sonia sat back smugly.

Hillary just smiled.

"Well? Write down my score—I'm whipping your butt!"

Hillary picked up the pen and threw it across the room. "Hey!" Sonia protested.

Hillary pouted at Sonia for a second. Then she balled up the page with the score and threw that too.

"I guess the game is over? Sore loser."

"Yes. I'll admit I am a better winner, but I'm getting a taste for something sweet." She smacked her lips.

"You cannot possibly be hungry again so soon. The dishes aren't even dry yet."

"I don't care. I'm craving something sweet and creamy."

"Ice cream?"

"Ummm . . . Nope. That's not it. Too cold. Hillary got up from her chair and sat on Sonia's lap, her hands reaching under Sonia's shirt.

"Pudding?" Sonia kissed Hillary's chest, burying her nose in Hillary's deep cleavage.

"Huh uh. Too fattening and too much trouble to wash the pot afterward." Hillary pressed closer, her hand massaging Sonia's neck.

"Well, what then?" Sonia's breath was warm, her words muffled between Hillary's breasts.

Hillary slid from Sonia's lap and knelt between Sonia's legs, parting her thighs. She ran her finger over the cotton crotch of Sonia's jockeys, feeling the heat beneath.

"Let's see . . . oooh, how about this—if it's rich and creamy." She kissed the damp spot at Sonia's center, and ran her thumb under the edge of Sonia's panties. "Mmmmm. Yes. Sweet, but with a tangy bite to it."

Using her nose, Hillary pushed the panties aside, and flicked her tongue in the juicy folds revealed.

Sonia's hands gripped Hillary's hair, gently scratching her scalp, her pussy jumping in response to Hillary's teasing tongue.

"Ummm . . . yes. This is the ticket. Want to taste?" Hillary lapped at the delicious moistness and then came up, kissing Sonia deeply, passionately as she worked Sonia's panties down over her hips and pushed them to the floor.

Sonia tasted her own arousal on Hillary's tongue and moaned with need as Hillary left her mouth and returned to Sonia's other plump, pouty lips.

Hillary buried her face in Sonia's tangled thatch of hair, enjoying the sensation of scratchy hair on her cheek that yielded to slick, smooth sweetness beneath. Thrusting her tongue into Sonia, she devoured the slippery dew pooled there and then carefully explored Sonia's luscious folds.

Sonia slumped back in her chair, clutching the arms for support, spreading her quivering thighs and gyrating her hips.

"Ah . . . ah . . ." was all Sonia could manage as Hillary slowly flicked her tongue over Sonia's swollen hood.

Hillary burrowed her face deeper into Sonia's nest, her fingers slipping into Sonia.

She drilled Sonia's dripping hole, her fingers covered in Sonia's oil. Her mouth locked on to Sonia's swollen clitoris as her tongue lashed swiftly over the hard nub. Sonia's thighs flexed, and realizing that Sonia was on the edge, Hillary twisted her hand and pumped her harder.

Sonia's body quaked, her pussy pulsating around Hillary's hand. Hillary quickly replaced her fingers with her mouth to better catch every drop of Sonia's eruption.

Hillary rested her wet cheek on Sonia's thigh, gently stroking Sonia's mound as her body calmed. Then, they finished their coffee and went to bed.

λ λ λ

After breakfast the next morning, Hillary convinced Sonia to take a hike in the woods. They laced up their boots and donned hats and gloves. Hillary filled a Thermos with hot chocolate and they headed out.

The air was brisk, but the sun was shining, the sky a clear, icy blue. They picked their way around muddy patches and over semi-frozen streams. Hillary pointed out green shoots and hearty little blossoms—early celebrants of spring.

They hiked for about an hour, finally stopping in a clearing where they sat on the trunk of a fallen tree and shared a cup of cocoa. It had gotten even colder and the sun was hidden behind dark, heavy clouds which had appeared from nowhere.

Sonia studied the sky. "I think we'd better get back—looks like a downpour."

Hillary looked up at the overcast sky. "Nah. We don't have to hurry. It's not going to rain. Smell the air—you can always smell the rain before it comes down. Trust me. I used to work at a summer camp as the nature specialist. I know all about these things."

Sonia looked dubious. "Okay . . . but as soon as we finish this cocoa, let's head back to be safe."

Hillary huffed scornfully. "City girls. Scared of a few little gray clouds. I'm telling you, it's not going to rain. But if you're gonna get hysterical, we'll go."

"I'll get hysterical." Sonia drained the cup and stood. "Let's go."

They were about ten minutes from the house when the sky opened up. They were drenched and shivering when they finally got inside.

"Okay, okay—so I was a little off—so sue me," Hillary said as they ran into the house, peeling off their sodden clothes. "Go take a shower while I make us some tea."

Sonia headed upstairs, muttering under her breath.

"Oh, quit your bitching. You'll live." Hillary shouted after Sonia. "For pete's sake. What a baby. I'll bring the tea up in a minute."

λ λ λ

Hillary made two mugs of Cranberry Cove tea, and as an afterthought, laced them liberally with rum and honey. She placed the cups and a plate of cookies on a tray and went upstairs.

Sonia had opted for the Jacuzzi. She lounged, dozing, in the hot, bubbling water. Hillary could smell the fragrant oils drifting up with the steam.

Setting the tray on the tub's edge, Hillary asked, "May I join you?"

Sonia indicated the space beside her. "I think we can make room for one more."

Hillary undressed and got in slowly, allowing her body time to adjust to the hot water. She was

finally able to sit with a long "Ahhhhh," as she settled.
Sonia handed her a mug. "Did you . . . ?"
Hillary took her cup. "Of course, honey. I made it just the way you like it." She watched Sonia take a sip. "Well?"
"Perfect. You've redeemed yourself."
"Oh, gee, thanks," Hillary said sarcastically as she sank deeper into the water, one foot brushing against Sonia's crotch suggestively.
"Has anyone ever told you that you are a raving sex-starved maniac?"
Hillary's foot explored further. "Yes. You did. That's why you fell in love with me."
"Oh yeah, that's right." Sonia shifted her body away from Hillary's aggressive toes. "But would you be offended if I took a rain check? I'm a little sleepy. Can we just relax for a few?"
"No prob. Don't mind me—it must be all this fresh air making me so horny." Hillary got up and leaned over the edge of the tub. The jets pulsed water on her pussy.
"Yup. Don't worry about me. We strong black wimmin know how to take care of ourselves." She moved her hips back and forth over the pulsing water.
Sonia's clitoris involuntarily responded to the vision of Hillary's lush, wet body, beads of water glistening on her mahogany skin like little diamonds. She loved watching Hillary play with herself.
From under half-lidded eyes, a mischievous smile at the corners of her mouth, Hillary watched Sonia. But the water called to her, her attention shifted to the spray pounding her pussy. She closed

her eyes, her body trembling as she moved closer to the jet stream.

Sonia couldn't bear it. Her body throbbed with the desire to ravage Hillary. She moved in, pushing Hillary up hard against the edge of the tub. Hillary moaned, the pulsing waters like a thousand fingers playing along her fevered crevice.

Sonia's hands were over Hillary's and the four hands milked Hillary's full, heavy breasts. Sonia suckled and nibbled Hillary's neck and shoulder as she rode Hillary's ass in firm, vigorous rotations.

Sonia leaned back, pulling Hillary with her. Hillary's legs opened, the distance from the jets now allowing the water to again have reign over her entire swollen pussy. Sonia reached a hand down and into Hillary's hole. Three wide fingers pummeled Hillary's pussy, while Sonia's hand and wrist rubbed up and down her pubic length.

Sonia's hot cunt ground hard against Hillary's ass, and Hillary moaned louder and louder as she succumbed to the feeling. "Oh god . . . oh god!" she chanted over and over as orgasm washed over her.

λ λ λ

The clock beside the bed read 2:43 a.m. and Sonia was wide awake. Hillary lay sleeping in the crook of her arm. Suddenly, Sonia sat up and reached for a cigarette.

Hillary stirred. "What's up honey?"

Sonia dragged deeply and blew the smoke up toward the ceiling before answering with a sigh, "Tomorrow we go home. Back to our busy lives."

Hillary sat up, putting her arms around Sonia's shoulder. "I know, the time flew by so quickly. Hasn't this has been a wonderful, wonderful weekend? A new beginning for us, sort of."

Sonia stood. "Is it? Is it really a new beginning? Has anything really changed?"

Hillary moved to Sonia. "This weekend was very important to me. It wasn't just about great sex—though I'm not complaining about *that*. It was about taking time out. Being good to myself—and *you* are good for me. I have to remember to keep things in perspective—I think you can help me with that. Won't you?" She kissed Sonia.

Sonia held her close. "I love you. Very, very much."

Hillary smiled. "Me too, you. Now let's get some sleep. We have a long ride back in the morning."

THE GATEWAY

Something bright flashed in Patrice's peripheral vision. Curious, she backed up, peering into the bare, ice-covered branches of the bush, but saw nothing. Maybe it was just the sun reflecting off the ice, she shrugged as she continued her morning jog.

The next morning, Patrice ran with her friend, Linda. The air was cold, invigorating. The two wimmin talked and laughed as they made their way down the deserted path. Patrice remembered the silver flash of yesterday, and as they came up on the bush, Patrice looked into the branches. The bush wavered like a mirage, almost translucent. Then, a sudden flash of silver. Patrice grabbed Linda's arm. "Did you see that?"

"What? See what?"

Patrice jogged over to the bush, reaching out a hand to touch the frozen branches. Gripping a twig, she watched the melting ice drip through her fingers.

"What's the matter? Hey—Pat!" Linda stopped beside Patrice, a look of concern on her face.

Patrice slowly withdrew her hand. "Ummm... nothing. It was nothing." Patrice smiled shakily. "I'll race you back to my place. Loser cooks breakfast!"

λ λ λ

The following morning, Patrice started out a little earlier and reversed her route. Coming up on the bush, she saw a figure kneeling on the ground. It was difficult to determine whether the person was male or female, dressed as it was in a padded bodysuit, only the face visible. The face was dark, blue-black like the night, and flawless. As Patrice came closer, the figure looked up and Patrice stopped in her tracks. The figure's eyes were a startling, vivid yellow. No pupils, just two glowing moons in a midnight face. The figure stood and, with a last look at the stunned Patrice, jumped into the bush.

Patrice waited a few seconds, but the creature did not reemerge, so she crept cautiously forward. Her heart was pounding as she moved closer, ready to run if there were any sudden movements. She peered into the bush. There was nothing there. Patrice walked around the bush. She saw footprints where the person had been, but none anywhere else. Despite the cold, Patrice broke into a sweat. She backed away down the path, not turning until the bush was no longer in sight. Then she ran like hell.

All day, Patrice contemplated the figure and the bush. What did it mean? She hesitated mentioning the experience—even to Linda—and risk being labeled a nut case with invitations to speak on talk shows. She needed incontrovertible proof. Of what? She didn't know. But she *had* to go back.

Patrice dressed warmly and left her house much earlier the next morning, her stride tense, cautious as she neared the park, camera slung around her neck. She felt ridiculous, like a bad actor in a B movie—the kind where the victim ignores the ominous music swelling and instead continues on to her certain doom.

Sitting on a bench behind a tree not more than ten yards from the bush, Patrice waited. Before long, the bush began to waver. Patrice rubbed her eyes and stared as a person stepped out of the bush and looked around. Patrice ducked behind the tree, removing the cap from the lens of the camera. The figure turned and moved away from the bush, making notes on a silver board. Patrice started snapping pictures as the being moved about, studying and recording.

Patrice had to get closer. Sliding off the bench, she inched around the tree and stepped on a twig, which snapped loudly in the cold, still air. The being turned, yellow orbs flashing. It looked to the bush, assessing the distance. Patrice made a sprint at the same moment, and when the being leapt into the bushes, so did Patrice. There was a flash of silver, and then blackness.

λ λ λ

When she awoke, Patrice was strapped to a table in a darkened room. Taking careful inventory of her body, she assessed that she not injured. "Stay calm" she chanted as her eyes adjusted to the gloom.

She could make out that she was in some sort of examination room. Her head was held loosely in a vise, but by straining her eyes to the right, she could make out a large console with dim, blinking, blue lights pushed up against the wall. It was perhaps four feet from the table she lay on, with dark wires running from it to—to her!

Cutting her eyes to the left, she made out a monitor, silently printing out data received from the wires she could now feel attached to her pulse points.

She had to be dreaming. What had happened? She tried to recall her actions before the blackout. Jumping into the bushes—and then—here. Suddenly there was a blinding, painful flash of silver. Patrice screamed, and passed out.

When she came to again, the being was beside her, adjusting the wires, studying the printout. Through half-lidded eyes, Patrice studied it. About five-foot-eight, it was slim, even under the silver padded suit it wore. The skin was indeed blue-black, gleaming and ageless. And it was flawless—except for a silver geometric etching running from its right eye to its hawkish nose. Its lips were full, sharp and black. But it was the eyes that drew Patrice. The eyes, framed by thick, silver brows and lashes, were luminescent, and Patrice gasped as she realized that the being's eyes were giving off the only light in the room.

There were no ornaments or designs on the uniform to give Patrice a clue as to where she might be. But she knew for damn sure, she wasn't in any hospital. And she knew that *it* was not human.

It turned to her. "Ah, Patrice, you are awake."

The voice was female. Soft, without inflection.

"How'd you know my name? Where am I? Why am I strapped to this table?" Patrice couldn't help the edge of hysteria creeping into her voice.

The—womon—touched Patrice's shoulder. The hand was cool and dry.

"I will answer all of your questions shortly, Patrice." She moved to the other side of the table and adjusted some knobs on the console.

Patrice strained against the restraints. "No! I want answers now, goddammit! I *demand* answers! Why am I being held here against my will? Who the hell are you?"

The being was unaffected by Patrice's tirade. In the same monotone voice, it answered, "I have been assigned to you, since it was my carelessness that brought you here. You will be studied and then released. You will not be harmed. But you must refrain from raising your voice aggressively again, or I will be forced to subdue you."

Patrice shivered. The words were calm, but the threat implied was clear.

"You went through the gateway before I could close it," the being continued. "I know your name because you carry identification. Where you are is difficult to explain. As I said, you will not be intentionally harmed. We simply wish to give you a series of tests and with the use of electronic impulses attached to your brain, we will monitor your physiological responses."

"No! I won't let you fuck with my brain! I'm not a guinea pig, goddamn it! Let me go! Let me—"

Patrice felt her body begin to warm and tingle. With a gasp, she felt her pelvic muscles begin to expand and contract. "Oh god! Oh God!!!" she yelled as a tremendous orgasm racked her body.

"Blood pressure, body temperature up, heartbeat and aspiration rate increased."

"What the hell—what are you doing to me?" Patrice panted as the spasms diminished.

"We are studying your species' sexuality. You humans are extraordinarily motivated by it."

This was too weird. Patrice dug her nails into her palms until it hurt. Yup. She was awake. She tried to recall all of the movies she had seen about UFOs and stuff like that. The heroes always got away by befriending the enemy and then outsmarting them. Okay. Okay. Let's try friendly.

"If I'm going to be kept here against my will, we may as well be properly introduced. You know my name—who are you?"

The being answered, "I am Xenobia."

"Xenobia. Okay, Xenobia. Why this fascination? Is what turns you on so different?" Patrice tried to make her voice sound suggestive. She chuckled, thinking to herself, "Do you come here often? What's your zodiac sign?" Stay focused, don't get hysterical, Patrice warned herself.

Xenobia turned to Patrice. "I do not understand this term *turn on*."

Patrice smiled archly. "Come on—what makes you hot—gives you pleasure. What, um—what makes your heartbeat and respiration rate increase?"

Xenobia answered, "We do not indulge in such primitive activities."

"Humph." Patrice grunted. "So in other words, you don't have sex." She mulled this over in her mind, an idea forming.

"I'd like to—" Xenobia turned a dial, cutting off Patrice's words as she was flooded with orgasmic sensations that seemed never ending, until Patrice screamed, tears falling from her eyes.

"Stop that! Why are you torturing me? You said you weren't going to hurt me!"

Xenobia leaned over Patrice, curiously touching the salty drops on her cheek. "I was not torturing you. I was giving you pleasure because you are cooperating."

"Endless orgasms may sound wonderful, but it's not! Orgasm after orgasm is too intense to be pleasurable."

A light bulb went on in Patrice's head. Well, she reasoned, she'd done kinkier things for less important reasons. Without missing a beat, Patrice said, "Orgasm is not the only goal or motivator of our sexuality, Xenobia. Why don't you let me up, so I can show you what I mean."

Xenobia considered for a moment, her eyes burning orange around the edges, and then loosened the restraints holding Patrice, helping her to a sitting position. There didn't seem to be any doors in the smooth, black walls. Shit. Patrice had better satisfy, if she was going to convince Xenobia to lead her out of this nightmare.

Shaking her limbs, Patrice stood and stretched. Then she turned to Xenobia. "Why don't you take off your suit. It's much nicer touching skin to skin."

Xenobia complied, unzipping her jumpsuit neck to waist. It fell silently to the floor. Xenobia stood before Patrice, now naked.

"Thank the Goddess, she's anatomically correct." Patrice sighed to herself. She studied Xenobia's body. It was pretty androgynous—small, high breasts, the nipples an electric blue against her perfect, black skin. Her hair, head and pubic, was short and also a vivid blue. She had tiny silver markings on her arms, legs, and belly—swirls and moons and stars.

Patrice generally preferred more fleshy wimmin, but she found Xenobia strangely erotic. "I really am out on the edge." She thought to herself as she reached out to touch the irresistible designs on Xenobia's thighs.

Xenobia stood, holding her clipboard, as Patrice trailed her fingertips over the strange grooves. Xenobia's body transmitted pleasant little electric shocks to Patrice. The currents ran through Patrice's fingertips and down to her pussy. Patrice was getting really turned on.

"What is the point of your actions, right now?" Xenobia asked as Patrice slid her hand between Xenobia's legs.

Patrice sighed irritably at the interruption, and took the clipboard, tossing it on the table. "Just pay attention. There will be a quiz immediately following. Now part your legs."

Xenobia did, and Patrice slipped her hand further into the mysterious folds. It felt human to Patrice—warm, damp. The scent though, that was different. Patrice manipulated Xenobia's slick cavern, and finding her clitoris, a small, hard kernel, Patrice stroked and flicked it. Her own pussy started to throb as she observed Xenobia's pubic hair turn a brilliant, electric blue with excitement.

Patrice slipped a finger into Xenobia, gripping and pulling her silky insides. Xenobia stood still, eyes closed, nostrils flaring, as Patrice slowly pumped her.

Patrice slipped in another finger, and then another. Each time she did so, Xenobia's hairs glowed brighter.

Patrice helped Xenobia to the floor and leaned over her, playing with the tiny blue buds on Xenobia's breasts as she twisted her hand inside Xenobia's tight orifice.

"Umph," Patrice grunted to herself, "I could fit my entire hand in here."

Working the rest of her hand, slowly, carefully up into Xenobia until her wrist brushed the flowing blue hairs, Patrice shifted her body until Xenobia's knee was positioned between her thighs, pressing hard against her throbbing pussy.

In the nocturnal light of the chamber, Xenobia's skin glowed. The silver markings on her body sparkled. Patrice closed her hand into a tight fist and began pumping Xenobia as she ground her own aching sex into Xenobia's leg.

Xenobia had forgotten Patrice, lost in the primal world of lust, long forgotten by her people. She rode Patrice's fist, rising up and slamming down as Patrice rocked her faster and faster.

Xenobia let out a high keen as her body buckled forward. Her eyes popped open, unseeing, now blood red. Xenobia clamped her muscles tightly around Patrice's fist inside her and pounded down on Patrice's slippery arm. Patrice felt Xenobia's skin heat up. The warmth spread to Patrice's body, quickening her pulse, her body tingling with the sensation.

Xenobia came, flowing like lava down Patrice's arm. Patrice fell to her knees, an orgasm swelling over her so strongly, she fainted.

When she awoke, Xenobia was standing over her, dressed again in her uniform. Patrice realized that she was also dressed in her jogging sweats.

"It is time for you to go. Please hurry, the gateway is open. We will be leaving here soon."

Patrice got up. "Back to—your home?"

Xenobia's eyes were yellow again, but flecked with bits of purple. "Yes. Now please hurry." Then she turned and walked to the wall, which slid open, revealing a dusky hallway. At the end of the corridor, Patrice could make out a hazy vision of the park. It was still early morning, by the light.

She turned to Xenobia. "So you go back to a world of dry science and no pleasure? I got the feeling you kinda liked being 'primitive'. Why don't you stay longer—we could do more research."

Xenobia's eyes pulsed. "Our studies have determined that your world is a violent, dangerous place."

Patrice took her hand. "Well, yes, it can be pretty scary, but it can also be a lot of fun—filled with exciting things to do and see and feel. You could always leave if you didn't like it. That's more than the rest of us can do."

"No. I would not be able to return home. I would become human. The gateway would be closed to me forever."

"That's rough." Patrice said quietly.

"Yes—rough." Xenobia became brisk. "Time is running out. Please. Just relax and walk through. You may experience some vertigo once you pass back into your world, but the feeling will fade. Goodbye—Patrice."

Patrice touched Xenobia's cheek. "Goodbye." Then she turned and walked into the light.

When the cold air hit her, Patrice staggered, dropping to her knees as a wave of nausea washed over her.

After a moment, she stood and looked at the bush. It wavered, not quite a mirage. Strangely, Patrice felt sad. She had kind of liked Xenobia. Ah well. An experience she would always remember and never be able to share at cocktail parties. She turned and started toward home.

At the bend of the road, she looked back. A flash of silver blinded her. When her vision cleared she saw—a figure—standing slowly, looking around. It was—yes! Xenobia! Patrice headed back toward her, and then stopped.

Xenobia had changed. Her skin had faded to a smooth, dark brown, the geometric etching on her cheek gone. Her eyes had dimmed to a soft, honey brown. She was breathtaking. Exotic. An African queen. She smiled at Patrice.

"I was hoping you might extend—how do you say—some 'down home' hospitality to a stranded sister."

Patrice laughed. "You're learning fast." She took Xenobia's hand and led her from the park.

Other Books from Third Side Press

STORIES

The Dress/The Sharda Stories   by Jess Wells.
Rippling with lesbian erotic energy, this collection includes one story Susie Bright calls "beautifully written and utterly perverse."   **$8.95   1-879427-04-4**

Two Willows Chairs   by Jess Wells.
Superbly crafted short stories of lesbian lives and loves.
$8.95   1-879427-05-2

The Country of Herself   Karen Lee Osborne, editor.
Questions of identity—cultural and personal—abound in this collection of short fiction by Chicago women writers, including Carol Anshaw, Sara Paretsky, Maxine Chernoff, Angela Jackson, and others.
$9.95   1-879427-14-1

NOVELS

The Sensual Thread   by Beatrice Stone.
The simple story of Leah Kirby's awareness of the beings on earth around her and how that love transforms her sense of self. Being empathic gives making love a whole new dimension.
$10.95   1-879427-18-4

Hawkwings   by Karen Lee Osborne.   A novel of love, lust, and mystery, intertwining Emily Hawk's network of friends, her developing romance with Catherine, and her search throughout Chicago for the lover of a friend dying of AIDS.
ALA 1992 Gay & Lesbian Book Award Finalist
$9.95   1-879427-00-1

Not So Much the Fall   by Kerry Hart.   Through a fog of angst and chemically-induced confusion, on an odyssey from Memphis to Portland—and back again nine years later—Casey glimpses the consequences of her life's actions.

> "This collage of one woman's life, memories, and twisted revelations takes readers on a road as winding as any Kerouac ever explored." —Nisa Donnelly

$12.95   1-879427-24-9

On Lill Street   by Lynn Kanter.   Margaret was a young, radical lesbian-feminist in the mid-1970s, her credentials unblemished, her ideals firm, when she moved to a mixed-gender house on Lill Street.

> "Watching everyone struggle with her/his feelings, politics, impulses is truly engrossing and a joyful experience." —Bay Windows

$10.95   1-879427-07-9

AfterShocks   by Jess Wells.   Tracy Giovanni had a list for everything, but when the Big One hit San Francisco—8.0 on the Richter scale—her orderly world crumbled.

> "This book kept me up all night."—Kate Millet

ALA 1993 Gay & Lesbian Book Award Nominee

$9.95   1-879427-08-7

DRAMA

She's Always Liked the Girls Best   by Claudia Allen.   Four humorous, heartwarming lesbian plays by two-time Jefferson-award-winning playwright.

ALA 1994 Gay & Lesbian Book Award Finalist
Lambda Book Award 1994 Finalist

$12.95   1-879427-11-7

MYSTERIES

Out for More Blood: Tales of Malice and Retaliation by Women Victoria A. Brownworth & Judith M. Redding, editors. Stunning sequel to the popular *Out for Blood* features gripping mystery stories of malice and retaliation by some of America's best new women writers. In these tales, ordinary events take extraordinary turns, with women at the nexus.
   Contributors: Amalia Pistilly, Beth Brant, Diane DeKelb-Rittenhouse, Helena Basket, J.D. Shaw, Joanne Dahme, Joyce Wagner, Judith Katz, Linda K. Wright, Lisa D. Williamson, Mabel Maney, Meredith Suzanne Baird, Nikki Baker, Ruthann Robson, Terri de la Peña, Toni Brown.
$12.95   1-879427-27-3

Out for Blood: Tales of Mystery and Suspense by Women   Victoria A. Brownworth, editor.
Fifteen previously unpublished stories by beloved and soon-to-be-beloved mystery writers. Tales of humor, terror, and otherworldliness, you'll find them creepy, scary, funny, nerve-wracking, horrifying, relieving, and memorable.

> "*Irresistible! From the evocative 'An Evening Out' by Victoria Brownworth to the delicious 'The Confectioner' by Meredith Suzanne Baird, this anthology sizzles and snaps with mystery and wit.*" —Ellen Hart

$10.95   1-879427-20-6

Timber City Masks   by Kieran York. Royce Madison is a major threat to some people in Timber City, Colorado. The question is, which people? The soft-spoken deputy could hardly be the kind of threat that the Family Morals Coalition claims she is, but as the only woman on the sheriff's department roster she has her work cut out for her.

In *Timber City Masks*, the first in the series, Royce must find the murderer of her lover's best friend and, in the process, explore her feelings about the death of her father in the line of duty.

$9.95   1-879427-13-3

Crystal Mountain Veils   by Kieran York. In *Crystal Mountain Veils*, second in the series, it's the murderer of gossip monger Sandra Holt that Royce Madison is after, and motive is the key: everyone hated the tabloid columnist, but who hated her enough to kill her, and why? $10.95   1-879427-19-2

BUSINESS

The Woman-Centered Economy: Ideals, Reality, and the Space in Between   Loraine Edwalds and Midge Stocker, editors. Principle-centered business and right livelihood? Feminists have been practicing them for 25 years. Creating and operating businesses and organizations based on personal beliefs is what the woman-centered economy is all about.

Sonia Johnson, Mary Kay Blakely, bell hooks, Phyllis Chesler, and others examine the women's community from an economic perspective, presenting case studies of real women's businesses and discussing how and why those businesses fail or succeed.

$15.95   1-879427-06-0

AUTOBIOGRAPHY

Enter Password: Recovery   Elly Bulkin
Autobiographical book about transforming the self through language. "A rich and challenging book, one that will inspire a lot of healing." —*Feminist Bookstore News* $7.95   1-879427-10-0

HEALTH

Cancer as a Women's Issue: Scratching the Surface   Midge Stocker, editor.   Very personal stories explore how cancer affects us as women, individually and collectively. Includes multiple perspectives on dealing with breast cancer.
  "*If you are a woman, or if anyone you love is a woman, you should buy this book.*"
  —*Outlines*
   Women/Cancer/Fear/Power series, volume 1
   $11.95   1-879427-02-8

Confronting Cancer, Constructing Change: New Perspectives on Women and Cancer
Midge Stocker, editor.   Confronting myths about cancer, presenting options for responding to a cancer diagnosis, and provoking political action to clean up the environment and reduce risks. Features writing by feminist cancer movement organizers around the U.S. and an introduction by Sandra Butler.
  "*Questions the usual, concealed reactions and advocates a more open, woman-centered, political stance.*" —*Booklist*
  "*Read it and reap.*" —*Chicago Tribune*
   Women/Cancer/Fear/Power series, volume 2
   $11.95   1-879427-09-5

Alternatives for Women with Endometriosis: A Guide by Women for Women   Ruth Carol, editor. Nutrition therapy, acupuncture, chiropractic, biofeedback, and massage therapy are a few of the available alternatives to relieving the pain of endometriosis without having a hysterectomy, taking toxic drugs, or getting pregnant when you don't want to.
"*I highly recommend you read this book. It can open some new doors for you.*"
—Endometriosis Association Newsletter
$12.95   1-879427-12-5

MENTAL HEALTH

SomeBODY to Love: A Guide to Loving the Body You Have   by Lesléa Newman.   Forty-two ways to rethink how you relate to what you eat and to people around you. Speaking from her own experience, Newman guides women toward a new view of ourselves, as beautiful, powerful, and lovable, regardless of our size or shape.
$10.95   1-879427-03-6

Beyond Bedlam: Contemporary Women Psychiatric Survivors Speak Out   Jeanine Grobe, editor.   Up-close and personal writing by women who have survived psychiatric abuse on psych wards and in mental hospitals.   **$15.95   1-879427-22-2**

Coming Full Circle: Honoring the Rhythms of Relationships   by Nancy VanArsdall. Personal, political, and spiritual, this guide works from the premise that to have healthy relationships we must honor the waxing and waning, the rhythmic cycles, in each of us and in our intimate relationships. In *Coming Full Circle*, VanArsdall examines the cycles of individuals as those cycles play into and intertwine in the cycles of relationships. The book's primary focus is on couple relationships, both heterosexual and lesbian, from a woman's point of view, with the author noting that "it is my contention that women do relationships."

> *"Years of perceptive insight and intuitive empathy as a therapist have provided Nancy VanArsdall with a deep understanding of the cycles of relationships. Now we can all receive the gifts of her wisdom on the pages of* Coming Full Circle.*"* —Merlin Stone

$15.95   1-879427-25-7

To order any Third Side Press book or to receive a free catalog, write to Third Side Press, 2250 W. Farragut, Chicago, IL 60625-1802 or call 1-800-471-3029. When ordering books, please include $2.50 shipping for the first book and .50 for each additional book.

Third Side Press
because every issue has more than two sides.

The book you are holding is the product of work by an independent women's book publishing company.